Slaying for SANTA

A FESTIVE & FILTHY TREAT

SARAH JD

Many thanks to my Alpha & Beta Readers: Anoesjka, Melissa, Gini, Heather, Tiffany, Arriana, Cheria, and my alpha & proofreader Jen.

 Formatted with Vellum

CONTENT WARNING

This story contains subjects that some readers may find triggering, and scenes that carry heavy warnings.

The details in this book are written for entertainment purposes and are dark romantic fiction. Some of the following things should not be attempted without educating yourself and your partner extensively while always practising safety and consent.

- Breath play (erotic asphyxiation: intentionally restricting or cutting off the oxygen to the brain for the purpose of sexual arousal) This can be dangerous if not done correctly.
- Extreme deep throating
- Sexual Sadism (Experiencing sexual pleasure from inflicting pain, suffering, or humiliation to others)
- Sexual Masochism (Experiencing pleasure from being humiliated, beaten, bound, abused, and receiving pain)
- Brutal fisting
- Somnophilia
- Biting

- Rough play
- Partner sharing (not why choose)
- Substance abuse & recovery
- Trafficking (not glorified)
- Kidnapping
- Killing & Graphic Violence

If you want
Santa to come...
be a good girl
and read the
book!

1

BELL

I jerk forward in my seat as the driver hits the brakes to see flashing blue lights up ahead.

"Uhhh, Miss. I think the police are at your destination." The driver's eyes flick up to his rearview mirror to lock with mine.

I just nod as the newsreader on the radio speaks of another victim being found in a Melbourne hotel room, pinning it on the serial killer they have dubbed, *The Seduction Slayer*.

Jesus, could they think of something with a bit more creative flair?

"I'll get out here," I state, unclipping my seatbelt and opening the door.

The driver rushes out too, popping the boot and retrieving my suitcase for me, standing it on the path.

"Have a good day. Enjoy your Christmas in Sydney." He smiles, and after enduring the crappy budget flight from Melbourne to Sydney, all I can manage is another nod.

And there it is. The frown.

I could tell him I'm smiling on the inside, but I think that will just confuse him more. People don't tend to understand people like me.

I'm too blunt. Too emotionless. Too honest. Too scary.

I actually don't mind that last one.

They should be scared.

The driver hurries back around his car, slipping in, and I glance up the road to the flashing lights.

Not exactly the welcoming I was expecting, but hey, I'm supercurious now.

As the share car speeds off the way we came, I slowly approach the house I'm meant to be spending Christmas in.

"Get off me!" a woman screeches, and other voices start yelling.

I can't see past the huge hedge that lines the boundary, but my ears pick up sounds of a scuffle. A grunt, and then feet running.

As I move in closer, I pop my head around the hedge to see a police officer chasing after a dark-haired woman as she runs around the back of the house.

Fucking hell. What am I about to walk into?

Taking out my phone, I ignore the rideshare notification asking me to leave a review, and open up my message thread with Tillie. If she's inside and there's some sort of drug raid happening, she should have at least given me a heads up.

I might be clean now, but one search on my name, and the cops will assume I'm tied up with whatever is going on in that house, given my long rap sheet of drug-related charges.

I frown when my eyes land on a message from Till that has nothing to do with why the police are here.

Great! How didn't I see this message earlier? It's time stamped six hours ago.

I haven't seen my best friend for a few months since she's been travelling. I only agreed to come here for Christmas so I could spend some extra time with her.

"Ouch, Mummy! You're hurting me!"

The high-pitched screech of a little girl has my head snapping back towards the house to see the mane of black hair that was fleeing from the officer before, rushing down the front steps, her hand fisted around the thin wrist of a beautiful little girl.

Libi.

Shit. That woman is Rhonda. Kit's batshit crazy ex-wife, and given the twist of pain contorting Libi's face, her mother is hurting her.

I'm about to intervene and step around the hedge when another figure comes rushing out the door, and for a moment, it's as if time slows.

Kitson Hall. Tillie's big brother has aged like a fine wine.

He's filled out even more since the last time I saw him, and certainly compared to the lanky guy that used to tease me when we were younger. Now he looks like he's carved for sin with those broad shoulders and rippling veins running up his tanned arms like live wires.

Well strip me bare and fuck me like a whore, I think I have a lady boner.

Too bad he's such a dick!

"Let go of her!" he growls, reaching out and snatching up Libi's other wrist, tugging her towards him.

Poor Libi cries out as Rhonda spins and yanks hard, their daughter now the rope in their tug of war.

"Give me more money and you can have the little bitch!" Rhonda snarls, her nasally voice grating on my nerves.

"Stop! Mummy, you're hurting me!"

Fucking hell. Can't they see what they are doing to that poor child?

Libi screams and cries, and it isn't until the police officers barrel out of the house too and rush for Rhonda that she lets go, only so she can run.

She doesn't make it more than two steps before one of the officers leaps on her, both of them tumbling to the driveway, while Kit sweeps Libi up in his arms and those tiny little hands cling to her daddy like she never wants to let go.

Fuck it. I knew coming here was a bad idea. It was bad enough when I knew Tillie and Dale would be here to be a buffer. But staying here alone, with Tillie's arsehole brother is a recipe for disaster.

I'll end up killing him. Literally. Not even kidding.

As the chaos outside the house continues, I take a step back and start walking in the other direction, hitting call on Tillie's name.

It rings for so long I'm about to give up when she finally answers.

"Hello?"

"Till... were you sleeping? Isn't it like the middle of the day there?"

Tillie yawns down the line. "Yeah... but we were up all night, and now we are holed up in a shitty motel with a shitty heater as the shitty weather gets even shittier. There's literally nothing else to do but sleep."

"Speak for yourself," Dale's voice comes down the line like

he's right next to her. "I could have been in the five-star hotel with the pilot, but noooo. Someone didn't want to be alone."

Tillie giggles at Dale's dramatics. "Shut up and go back to sleep."

"Hi Dale!" I call into the receiver.

"Hey bitch. Enjoying the Aussie summer yet?"

I snicker at Dale. "Well, the fact that I'm wearing a little black summer dress and you're practically hugging a heater, I'm gonna say yes, I am enjoying the summer. What better way to spend Christmas?"

Tillie scoffs. "You don't even like Christmas."

"True, but if I have to choose between Christmas in the snow, or Christmas on a beach, you know which one I'm choosing."

"Bitch. I'm going back to sleep to dream of a beach," Dale whines.

"So... how's Libi? Did you hug her for me?"

I sigh. "No hugs, no."

"What? Why?"

I glance back over my shoulder as I hear car doors slam shut.

"Me and your brother under the same roof unsupervised will end up like Nightmare on Elm Street... for him."

Tillie laughs. "Don't be so dramatic. You are both adults now. Surely you can get along for a few days until I figure out how to make a spell that stops a blizzard."

"I just think it's a better idea if I find a hotel to stay in. A five-star hotel with room service and a pool and—"

"Okay, now you're just being mean." Tillie huffs, causing the speaker to crackle. "Please stay with Kit. He really is expecting you. And you know why he is the way he is. It's nothing personal. Besides, he's changed over the last couple of years since booting Rhonda to the curb. He has a little girl to raise now. His affliction with women has eased."

"I doubt that, Tills," I remark, turning to watch the police car reverse out of the driveway with Rhonda in the back. "His demons and my demons... they don't play well."

"Pleeeaseeee," she begs, and I roll my eyes.

"Fine. I'll try. But don't blame me when you get a call saying he's been gutted like a fish and strung up by his intestines."

"Hehe. I look forward to it."

For a moment, I feel myself smiling... on the inside, of course.

"Well, gotta go and start annoying the hell out of your big brother. Enjoy the snow."

Tillie starts whining again, but I hang up, knowing she won't be offended.

She knows me. How I am. Not to take it personally.

I stand on the path outside a neighbouring house for a moment contemplating if I should ignore what I just said to Tillie and find myself a hotel.

But shit, I'm bored, and annoying Kit is fun, so maybe it won't be so bad.

Making my decision, I walk back towards the house, pulling my bag up the small incline of the driveway before lifting it up the eight steps.

And yes, I counted. There are exactly eight.

The house... or rather mansion, it's a mix of stone and render with dark framed windows, giving the exterior an expensive yet rustic feel.

The front door is huge. Wide and tall, painted black, with a Christmas wreath in the centre. Before I knock, I peek through the glass panel next to the door to see the rustic mood flows inside too, with dark raw timber framing the doorways and staircase, the walls a deep navy, almost black.

Shit. Kit has taste.

I'm about to knock when I spot a doorbell, so I press that instead, and a second later, a Christmas carol chimes inside.

My lips tug up. Holy shit. Kit is into Christmas.

The door swings open rather aggressively, and a bare-chested Kitson Hall stands before me, rippling muscles up his arms and well... most of what I can see, exuding strength and something a little more lethal given the deadly style of the ink travelling up one arm and disappearing over his shoulder.

"What?!" he snaps, his blue eyes, just like his sister's, glaring at me with rage storming in them as some of his auburn hair falls in his eye. "Oh... sorry. I thought you were someone else." He clears his throat, the anger falling from him like a switch has been flipped. "Can I help you?"

My lips are still turned upward in a slight smile, something that I don't often do, but shit, this really is too amusing. He doesn't even recognise me.

"I dunno, Kitty Kat. Can you help me?"

I pop my hip, crossing my arms over my chest, and I know he's trying super hard not to look at my tits as my words sink in. And then, his nice guy persona falls away like he's shed his skin, and his expression turns hard as a sinister smirk kicks up his lips.

"Belladonna."

KIT

"That's not my name, Kitty Kat, and you know it," she deadpans, and fuck, Bell Bishop is a sight for sore eyes. Not that I'd ever admit that to her. She'd probably slit my throat just for trying to be nice.

She looks... different. Definitely not the same kid I knew a couple of years ago.

"Belladonna is fitting though. Right?" I wag my brows knowingly, and if she were anyone else, like my ex-psychotic-wife for example, she'd get angry. Maybe even throw a fit.

But no. Not Bell Bishop. This chick is a different kind of crazy, and she soaks in insults like they are fucking compliments.

"You been reading my files again, Kitty?"

My smirk falls away at her words. "How many fucking times do I have to remind you to call me Kit or Kitson?"

She shrugs. "It's a waste of breath. Just like Belladonna is fitting for me, Kitty is fitting for you... since you are such a *pussy*." She pops the 'p' and her hand whips out, and before I know what's happening, she shoves me.

I stumble back, watching as she grabs the handle of her

suitcase, and strolls into my house like she fucking belongs here.

"Where's Libi?" she asks, leaving me staring blankly for a moment at how fucking good she looks.

The goth girl she wore like armour as a teen is gone, and in its place is something more... fuck. Hot. Sexy. Fucking tempting.

She stops in her tracks the moment she spots the chaos in the living room, and her eyes, normally hard, flick back to me with concern in them.

"What happened?"

"Rhonda," I mutter as I step closer, my eyes tracking the black inked vines and red flowers that paint her décolletage, trailing up her neck to finish just under her jaw, and across to her shoulders, weaving down her upper arms.

Her dark lashes aren't painted with thick mascara like she used to wear, but she doesn't even need it since the long fan of them are pitch black as it is. Her brown eyes look more like whiskey than chocolate in this light, accentuated with a brush of black liner, and her midnight hair, which used to be long, sits just on her shoulders in messy waves, some of it pulled into a loose ponytail on each side, with the rest down at the back, some loose strands framing her face.

That, and the way the black dress with little red flowers clings to her slender curves, is distracting enough, but then there are those fucking lips.

Fuuuck. They're a dusty rose colour, plump, but not the fake kind of plump, and fuck, they look so soft and—

"When you're done ogling, can you tell me where Libi is?"

Her words are like a bucket of ice, and I fucking stagger back a step, shaking my head to clear my fucking thoughts.

Fuck's sake, man. Get a grip!

"She's over in the corner, near the tree," I mutter, nodding my head in that direction, and for a long moment, Bell stares at me, tilting her head to the side in that creepy way of hers.

It makes me squirm. It's like she's trying to peer into my soul. To see all of my dark depraved secrets. The good and the bad. And fuck. There are so many bad ones.

"Where's your shirt?" she asks, surprising me.

"On the couch."

"And why isn't it on?" She quirks a single dark brow.

"Rhonda tore the fuck out of it."

She gives me a single nod before turning away from me and abandoning her suitcase to step into the living room.

Her eyes track over everything, like she's memorising every detail, and it's only now that I notice the blaring music is still flowing from the TV that is half hanging off the wall.

Stepping over some broken glass and splinters of wood from the picture frame Rhonda threw around in her hissy fit, Bell rounds the couch and stills the moment her eyes land on Libi.

Shit. I don't even know what to do. My little girl is inconsolable right now.

"Turn that shit off," Bell snarls over her shoulder at me.

I want to tell her not to fucking order me around, but then I see the way Libi is tucked against the wall, rocking herself with her hands over her ears.

Shit. I should've known this would induce an episode.

I hurry to find the remote, but it's nowhere in sight, so I step over more broken glass and flick off the power point, shutting the Christmas carols off instantly.

"Lights," Bell says in a hushed tone, and I meet her gaze. "Can you dim them or turn them off?"

I nod, moving to the dimmer switch, and lower the brightness, my eyes finding hers until she nods.

With the soft glow settling over the room, I want to kick myself for not fucking acting sooner to help Libi. She prefers lower lighting. Especially when she's stressed. Same with loud noises.

Fuck it! My head isn't in the right fucking place right now.

Fucking Rhonda!

"Hey, Libs." Bell's voice takes on a soft tone, unlike I've ever heard from her, and shit... does this woman who was voted Most Likely to Become a Serial Killer by her peers at school, actually have a soul?

Lowering to the floor next to my daughter, Bell positions herself similarly to Libi, gaining her attention, and my daughter slowly stops rocking, her tiny hands falling from her ears.

"Bell?"

Her voice is so fucking soft, her big blue eyes locking with Bell's in wonder.

Fuck. They are so similar. Bell and Libi almost look like mother and daughter with the same dark hair, big eyes, although a different shade, and well, they have similar mannerisms. I've tried to ignore how similar they are in personality. The quirkiness. The bluntness. The like of all things dark and creepy.

Sometimes I think my daughter was born in a horror movie. Sure, she likes dolls, but only if they can wear black clothes with skulls on them.

Shit. That reminds me of why Rhonda flipped the fuck out.

The Christmas tree.

"Hi, Libi," Bell coos quietly. "I thought I'd come and annoy your dad for Christmas. Is that okay with you?"

Libi giggles and nods. "Yes. You annoy him a lot."

I stiffen, but not because of what Libi said. It's because Bell's lips kick up in a fucking smile. Not the quirk of the lips she gifted me at the front door before, but this smile... I've never seen her smile like that.

It's broad, and she actually looks... happy.

"I know." Bell bops Libi on the nose, and my little girl giggles again. "Annoying your dad is so much fun."

Libi's joy is short-lived as she glances over her shoulder at the Christmas tree strewn over on its side, her smile falling away.

"Hey, what's the frown for?" Bell asks, drawing my daughter's attention again, and her big eyes peer up at Bell with so much trust in them.

It may have been a few years since I've seen Bell, but it's only been a few months since Libi has seen her. They usually catch up every time Tillie takes my daughter for a weekend so I can have a little break, but Bell and I deliberately avoid running into each other, so I haven't seen her in... well... years.

On my part, it's mainly so I don't lose my shit in front of Libi since Bell knows how to push my fucking buttons. I assume Bell's reason is the same.

We just don't play well.

"The tree is ruined," Libi says softly, tears welling in her beautiful blue eyes.

"We can fix it. Or get a new one," Bell offers, and shit, Libi's eyes go round in excitement despite the big fat tears popping from them.

"We can get a new one?" she asks before she looks excitedly around for me. "Can we, Daddy? Please, can we get the one I want? Pleeeease."

Sighing, I rake my hand through my hair knowing this won't go down well with Rhonda, but since she's just been carted to lockup for the night, and this is *my* fucking house, not Rhonda's, I guess we can get the tree that started all of this.

"Sure, Libs. We'll go first thing in the morning and get it."

Libi goes still, and for a moment, I think my little dark angel has stopped breathing, but then she bursts up from the floor, climbing over the couch like it's Mount Everest, and throws herself into my arms.

"Thank you, Daddy! Thank you!"

I wrap my arms around my little girl, squeezing her tight as she clings to me like I'm her whole world, and my eyes meet Bell's as she stands.

'*Thank you,*' I mouth, and I expect a nod or something. But instead, Bell's dark eyes remain locked on mine as she rounds the couch and saunters past me, her voice low.

"You can thank me later."

Fuck… why does that sound like an invitation?

I spend the first couple of hours at Kit's helping him and Libi clean up the mess Rhonda made. I didn't want to ask any more about what happened with Libi around, but now that she's finally sound asleep, I'm about to find out what in Satan's fiery hell I walked into here.

Stepping into the lush kitchen with the same warm rustic vibe as the living room, I find Kit at the sink, washing a few dishes, this time wearing shorts and a tank like he's about to hit the gym.

My eyes flick briefly to the muted TV on the wall with more headlines about The Seduction Slayer flashing across the screen.

They make it sound like a bloody vampire slayer or something. Like what's wrong with the Siren Stalker, or the Goth Widow? Or even the Kiss of Death Killer?

I roll my eyes at myself for even caring about that shit, and drag my attention back to Kit, and the red belly black snake ink winding from under the strap of his tank to coil up the back of his neck.

Shit. I didn't notice that earlier.

Hell's bells, get your head out of the gutter, woman!

"I've come to collect my thank you." I force myself to speak as I approach the black stone island bench between us.

Kit's head whips over his shoulder like I scared him, some of the water sloshing over the sink to trickle to the floor.

"Fucking hell, Bell. I know you don't have a fucking soul, but could you not walk around here like a fucking ghost? Make some damn noise when you enter a room."

I hitch a brow. "Sure, Kitty. I can do that."

He rolls his eyes and turns his attention back to the soapy water, reaching in and pulling the plug out before shaking the suds off his hands and drying them with a hand towel.

"Don't you have staff for that?" I nod my head towards the sink as he turns, and he shrugs.

"Gave them the night off since Satan was going to be here. They don't get paid enough to deal with her shit too." He leans back against the sink, crossing his arms over his chest. "So, how exactly do you want me to thank you?"

The way his brow quirks has me chewing the inside of my mouth to stop the smile that wants to appear.

I've already smiled twice since arriving. That's enough for one day.

"Tell me what the hell happened with Rhonda. Why was she even here?"

His auburn brow lowers, and he pushes off the bench. "Not really your business, Belladonna."

"Of course. I should've known you were too much of a pussy to be honest with me." I roll my eyes and spin on my heel, heading for the door.

I only make it a few steps before a firm hand grips my arm and spins me around to come face to face with the top of Kit's heaving chest.

I forgot how tall he is. Or at least, how tall he is compared to my nearly five ten height. He'd be at least six five. Maybe six six.

"You don't know shit about me, Bellicent."

My brows hitch, and for a moment I'm certain I stop breathing.

He said... my real name. The name only my mother used.

I part my lips to speak, but no words form, and he doesn't miss a beat, a smirk kicking up his lips that shouldn't look as tempting as they do framed by the dark auburn speckled stubble dusting his jaw, chin, and upper lip.

"What's wrong? Cat got your tongue?"

"I don't know, Kitty Kat... do you?" I ask quietly, and his grip loosens on my arm, but he doesn't step away, his searing hand remaining in place.

For a long moment, he just stares at me, and usually I'm good at reading people, but right now, I can't tell what's going through his head.

Then, his gaze flicks to my lips, and I swear time slows, and then completely stops.

Kiss me...

Wait!

Fuck!

No!

I take a step back, wrenching my arm from his grip.

"Why did your ex-wife trash the living room?" I snap, and he sighs, his shoulders dropping in defeat as he steps away, putting what feels like worlds of space between us.

"I agreed to let her come over so Libi could give her the Christmas gift she made her." Kit sighs, raking his hand through his hair, making some of the strands stick straight up. "Libs had been hounding me for weeks, and fuck, I thought I'd better get it over and done with so she would stop fucking bugging me about it. Then at least we could forget about her bitch of a mother and enjoy Christmas in peace." He huffs out a breath, turning away from me to brace the bench and drop his head like he's exhausted.

All I can see is the way his muscles coil.

Fuck me. What is wrong with me tonight?

"Took me long enough to get that cunt of a woman to show her face. I had to bribe her with twenty K just to come and see her kid for Christmas. Should've known she'd ask for more as soon as she stepped foot inside again." He shakes his head before lifting it and turning back to face me. "I should've lied to Libs and told her Rhonda was out of the country or something."

"So why did she go off? Was it just about the money?" I ask, and Kit's jaw ticks, clearly still frustrated with what happened.

"Rhonda is always money driven. She snorts most of it up her fucking nose. But the other thing that riles that woman up is how different our daughter is." Anger flares across his expression as he shakes his head. "Libi gave Rhonda the gift she made at school. She painted her a Christmas tree. The tree she really wants more than anything, thinking her mum would like it too."

"What's wrong with that?" I ask confused, and Kit growls.

"Rhonda didn't fucking like it."

I frown. "Why?"

For a long moment, Kit just stares at me like he's trying to figure out what to do, then he sighs again, moving to the drawer and pulling out pieces of torn paper.

He starts laying them out on the counter, piecing them together like a puzzle, and my brows shoot up as a painted Christmas tree starts to form.

It's no ordinary Christmas tree though, and my eyes meet Kit's as he steps back after putting the last piece into place.

"She told her mother that this is the tree she wants, and that she has these cute little skeletons and skulls to hang on it." He shrugs. "I guess this was just another thing Rhonda can't stand about her own daughter."

"All of that over Libi wanting a black Christmas tree? With skulls?"

Kit nods again.

"Can I kill her?" I deadpan, and his lips kick up as he chuckles.

"She's not worth it."

"I disagree." I want to add that any mother that squeezes their child's wrist like I saw deserves to have their hands cut off, but then I'll have to explain that I witnessed more than I'm letting on, and while I'm typically honest, I do know that withholding information is sometimes necessary. "I'll drag it out if you like."

His eyes narrow as he stares at me. "I can't tell if you're being serious or not."

"Have you known me to joke?"

"No, never."

"Well. There's your answer." I shrug.

"So you did it then?" he asks, turning away and moving to the fridge.

"Did what?"

"Became the serial killer everyone expected you to be," he states, so matter-of-factly as he opens the fridge and reaches in, snagging two cans of beer.

"What would you say if I said yes, that's exactly what I became?"

Straightening, his head darts over his shoulder, some auburn strands falling in his eyes again, which must annoy him, because he bats them away.

"I think I should ask if I'm your next victim?"

"Depends."

"On what?" His voice rises like he's actually worried.

"If you've done something worth being killed for."

His lips kick up. "Who decides what's worth it and what isn't?"

"Well me. Duh." I roll my eyes. "I'm the killer."

He throws his head back laughing, and again, I fight the urge to smile.

What the hell...

"This is a weird fucking conversation." He strides towards me holding out one of the beers.

"Pass," I say, shaking my head, and he frowns.

"I don't have harder stuff than beer in my home," he states almost angrily, like I'm the one doing something wrong.

I suppose the me three years ago would have already had a few lines of coke by now.

"I'm sober. No drugs or alcohol for me," I admit, like it's no big deal, but by the way his brows shoot up, I know he's going to make it a big deal.

"Bell... that's fucking amazing." He moves back to the fridge, and I hold my hand up to stop him.

"Let's not make a big thing about it."

He puts both cans of beer back in the fridge and turns to face me. "Why the fuck not? It is a big thing. A huge fucking thing. How long have you been sober?"

I shrug, feeling awkward, the sensation unfamiliar to me. "A while."

"Hey." He steps up to me, both hands gripping my upper arms, his blue gaze locking with mine, and I stiffen, waiting for the urge to flee that normally comes when people crowd me. "I know you know the exact day count, Bell. One of my mates is sober too. When I saw him a few days ago, he was on day four hundred and thirty-seven. What's yours?"

I don't know why this is a big deal. Not for him, but for me. It's like the words refuse to come, because the only people I ever say my day count to are myself, my therapist, my sponsor, and in group meetings. I don't even tell Tillie, and she never asks.

"Please tell me," Kit urges, and I frown.

"Why? So you can use it against me?" I snarl, and he quickly frowns.

"The fuck," he snaps, and I think he's going to shove away from me, but his hold only gets tighter. "I would *never* ever do that. Not for something so important. I may be a prick of a person at times, but with this, I will never dishonour it."

My heart is racing. I don't know why it feels like it's ready to steam train out of my chest, but it sure feels ready to take off at any second.

Another sensation washes over me, and I feel a sense of safety and peace here in this moment, so I hardly notice when my lips part and I speak.

"Nine hundred and nineteen days."

His lips part this time, and then they slowly spread wider until his face is engulfed in his smile.

"Nine hundred and fucking nineteen days?"

I nod, and he scoops me up, spinning me around while he laughs.

"Nine hundred and nineteen!" he cheers, and I'm certain he's lost his mind.

In the seven years I've known him, never once have we touched this much, let alone had more than five sentences said to each other, and when we did speak, the words weren't very pleasant.

For a beat, I feel light, and a little giddy, which is strange, because I usually only feel that way when I'm high on drugs, or from a fresh kill. And then, of course, there's the few times where I've lingered on the edge of life while having my air cut off during sex. That's one high I haven't had in a while.

My feet land on the floor again as Kit puts me down, and we stumble back from each other.

His smile is still huge, and I can't help but smirk, watching him take me in.

"Damn. You're so different."

"Stop looking at me like that," I deadpan, trying to get this interaction back on track.

The track being he despises me and we butt heads.

"Stop looking at you like what?" he asks, and I shrug, knowing all I can do is be honest.

"Like you want to fuck me." I cross my arms over my chest, and his eyes drop to my cleavage.

"I do want to fuck you," he states without a lick of shame, and I scoff.

"You hate me."

"Exactly." His blue eyes flick back to mine. "It's called hate fucking. Probably the best fuck you'll ever have."

I roll my eyes. "You must enjoy hate fucking Rhonda then." I point out, and he cringes, his face screwing up as he shakes his head.

"Fuck no. If I stick my cock in her, it will drop off." He shudders. "In fact, I'd rather become a eunuch."

A laugh bursts from me, and I slap my hand over my mouth as we both stare at each other in shock.

"What the fuck is happening?" he asks. "You just laughed. I don't think I've ever heard you make that sound before."

"Uhhhh. Same." I deadpan, frowning at myself as my hand falls away from my lips. "Maybe I need to go to a meeting."

"Fuck that." Kit shakes his head quickly. "Do you feel like you need a drink right now?"

I shake my head at Kit's question.

"Then why would you need to go to a meeting?" he asks. "Come up to my room, I'll make you feel better."

Fuck, is that a blush? Did I really just make the cold and unemotional Bell Bishop blush? And laugh!

Fuck, I'm on a roll.

"We can't fuck. Libi is asleep upstairs," she remarks, taking a step back from me, so naturally, I take a fucking step forward, because she's shit outta luck if she thinks this isn't happening.

"Libi sleeps like the dead," I counter, watching Bell take yet another step back as she scoffs.

"Well, I fuck like the world is ending, so she will definitely wake up."

My lips spread wide in a grin.

There's one thing you can always count on from Bell Bishop.

Brutal honesty.

"Fuck, Belladonna. I bet you're freaky in the sheets." I take two steps closer this time as she moves faster.

"You can't handle my kind of freaky, Kitty Kat." Her dark brow quirks, and I can tell she actually believes that.

"Shall we make it a bet? Because I'm pretty sure I'll surprise you. I like to get pretty fucking filthy."

Her feet stop, and so do mine as we stare at each other. She wears such a neutral expression it makes it hard to read her, but the moment I dart my tongue out to wet my lips, her eyes track the movement, and her breathing quickens.

"You're thinking about it, aren't you?" I smirk, and those pretty whiskey eyes flick back to mine.

"Shut up."

Huh! I fucking knew it!

"Come on, let's go." I step forward and grab her wrist, but she yanks it free, shaking her head.

"No, Kit. I can't."

She just called me Kit. Not Kitty. Not Kitty Kat. Not pussy cat. Just Kit.

I shouldn't fucking like it, yet I do.

"Why not?" I ask, standing in her personal space, so close she has to crane her head back to see my face. "You on your monthly? I don't mind blood. In fact, blood, bodily fluids... it's all a part of the filthiness I fucking love."

Her lips part as she peers up at me past her midnight lashes, her top teeth popping out to bite into her lower lip.

Fuuuck. She likes the sound of that.

"That's not why," she breathes after releasing her lip, her voice soft and a little husky.

"Then why?" I ask, stepping flush with her, reaching up to comb my fingers into her hair, and fuck... it feels just like silk.

She doesn't fight me. Doesn't push me away. In fact, I'm pretty sure she fucking melts against me.

"You're Tillie's brother." She states the obvious. "She's my best friend."

"Not a good enough excuse, Bell. It doesn't change anything for me." My free hand grips her hip, and fuck, she's still such a skinny thing. I can feel the bones of her hip under her little dress. "I still wanna fuck you. It's just sex."

She scoffs, shoving me back, and even though I could fight it, I don't, letting my hands fall away.

"Men say that all the time and guess what? They get clingy." She rolls her eyes like all men are pathetic. "Guess what I *had* to do to make them stop?"

My brows shoot up at her implication.

If she were anyone else, I'd say she's implying she hurt them to try to scare me. But this is Bell fucking Bishop. It's no implication. It's the fucking truth.

"Did you make them scream, Belladonna? Make them bleed?"

"Of course." She shrugs, like it's a no brainer.

"What if I promise you can kill me if I get clingy?"

"I don't need your permission to kill you, Kitty. If I want you dead, then dead you will be."

My cock jerks at her words. I typically consider myself an alpha male. Hell, I sure as shit played that role in my platoon years ago, but the thought of this woman taking a knife to me and slicing my skin open... Fuck. I'm as hard as stone.

"So really, what you're saying is that you like me. Otherwise, I'd be dead."

She rolls her eyes again. "You're an idiot, Kitson Hall." She spins on her heel. "I'm going to unpack."

"But you don't even know what room is the guest room," I snap, feeling annoyed that she's leaving me here to deal with the fucking seven-inch monster tenting my fucking pants.

"I can find it," she calls, disappearing down the hall, and I have to fucking fight the urge to chase after her like a fucking desperado.

What the fuck is wrong with me?

This is Bell. The emotionally damaged girl who used to wear her hair in two braids, with high collared dresses, every stitch of clothing black.

She was a Wednesday Addams lookalike if I ever saw one.

I know all about her past. I read the files she shared with me when I asked where she came from the third time Tillie brought her home from school and fed her dinner. She carried those damn files around like a security blanket, but I quickly learned when she handed them to someone to read over, it meant she trusted them.

She couldn't say the words out loud, I guess. So she let me read all about her upbringing. The house she grew up in with her mother... and her father. How every night at eight o'clock, her dad would send her to bed, while she had to listen to him rape her mother.

Then, once that was done, they were both locked into the small section of the house that had no windows, where they would stay until he came to let them out at five in the afternoon the next day.

He'd made them his slaves, and up until Bell escaped when she was close to thirteen, she'd never seen another child, let alone kids her age. She only knew one life up until then, and she'd been conditioned to be emotionless, because showing emotions meant punishment, and her punishments were brutal.

"Tillie is the only person who understands me," she said with her typical neutral expression when she was just fourteen years old. "So here are my files. Here's what's wrong with me, and why I'm different. I know you want to protect your little sister, but just so you know, I want to protect her too."

She'd told the truth. She'd been doing that for years. Protecting Tillie. So when I enlisted in the Australian Army, I knew my little sister would be okay until I could make something of myself and come back to her.

Shit. Bell Bishop.

She's always been an anomaly I couldn't understand.

Mainly, the way I was drawn to her.

Raking my hand through my hair, I turn back to stare at the painting Libi had done for her mother.

She wanted a black Christmas tree. It wasn't the first time she asked for one. She's been asking for it for the last two years. So, fuck Rhonda. If she's gonna come in here, throw my stuff around because she thinks our daughter has the devil in her, then she can go get fucked.

Libi is getting that fucking black Christmas tree, tomorrow fucking morning.

Gathering up the torn paper, I slip it back into the drawer and flick the lights and TV off before moving through the ground floor of my house to double check the doors and windows are locked. I key in the pin for the alarm system, and turn to face the stairs.

Light flows down from upstairs as I take the steps, two at a time. The landing light is on, and the door to the guest room, right next to Libi's room, is wide open.

I peer in, only all I find is Bell's suitcase sitting unopened on the end of the bed.

Where the fuck is she?

Glancing at the open bathroom door, I notice the light inside is off, which means she's not in there... And there's no light coming from under Tillie's door... so where is she?

My eyes drift to the second staircase that goes up to my private quarters. My home office is up there, plus a small living area and my bedroom with an attached bathroom and dressing room.

Is it extravagant? Yep, it sure the fuck is, but considering we grew up with nothing, and I've worked fucking hard to provide, not just for my daughter, but my little sister, and unbeknownst to Bell, her too, I think I fucking deserve some luxury.

Moving up to the third floor, I find my office door wide open, but the room empty, so I check the living room, and then my bedroom, where I find Bell opening my bedside drawer.

"What are you doing?" I snap, but she doesn't even flinch at the sudden sound of my voice.

"Snooping. Obviously."

"Obviously," I snap, rushing in, because I know what's in that fucking drawer, but it's too fucking late.

Bell turns to face me with the fucking thing in her hand before I make it another step.

"Does this get much action?"

"Put it down," I growl, storming towards her, but she simply shakes her head.

"I'd like a demonstration."

"I'm not demonstrating anything. If you want to see my cock slide into a set of lips, you can fucking volunteer and watch in the mirror." I gesture to the floor to ceiling mirror running along the wall next to one side of my bed, and, fuck me, but her brow quirks up, a look of curiosity flicking over her expression.

"How far down do you like to go?"

Jesus... does she mean...

"Down the throat?" I ask, and she nods.

"I need to know if we're compatible. If I'm going to open my mouth for someone, then it'd better be worth it."

"How far do you want me to go?" I step closer and snatch the silicone mouth from her, and the fucking thing starts talking.

. . .

"Ohhh yes, Santa. Just like that. Choke me with your big cock, Santa."

Bell sucks in her lips, trying not to laugh, which I might fucking add, is a hard feat to make her do. I flip the damn switch off and toss the fucker back into the drawer.

"Uh, uh, Santa. I asked you first." Her lips kick up in a smirk as she presses one of her sharp red claws into the centre of my chest. "How do you like to fuck a mouth? Because there are a few different ways, and I want to know exactly what you picture in your head when you fuck that thing... are those lips meant to belong to Mrs Clause?"

She bobs her head in the direction of the fuck toy, not an ounce of fear or shame on her face about this fucking conversation or the fact I have a silicone mouth that sucks and talks to Santa.

Fuck my life.

Sighing, I try to focus on what the fuck is happening here.

"You want to know what I imagine?" I ask, pushing the drawer shut in case the fucking thing starts talking again. "Or what I do with other women?"

There goes that fucking dark brow again.

"I want to know exactly what you *wish* you could do with women, but don't, for whatever reasons... usually fear of rejection... so instead you imagine it when you fuck Mrs Clause's mouth."

I fucking smirk, biting back a laugh.

"No one's ever asked me this before." I clear my throat... fuck, is it getting hot in here?

Bell nods. "Likely no one will because most chicks are too scared of what their partners' fantasies might mean for them. But I'm not like other women. I actually like it rough. I like being abused." She shrugs one shoulder like that's no big deal and drops her arse down on my bed. "Most guys get scared of the things I'm willing to let them do to me."

Fuuuuuuuuuuuuuuuuuck!

Is she the one? You know, the one that matches how fucking kinky I am. How depraved I can be. How fucking disturbing I've become.

Is she the one... one?

My fucking heart does this weird flip in my chest that I've never fucking experienced before, and either I'm about to go into cardiac arrest, or Bell Bishop has kickstarted the fucking thing.

"If I tell you, not a word of it gets shared with my sister." I jab a sharp finger in her direction, and Bell rolls her eyes.

"Trust me. Till's learned years ago not to ask questions. She knows I'm into fucked up stuff, and she still loves me anyway."

"She knows some of the stuff you've done?"

Bell nods. "Some of it. She just begs me to be safe... since you know, some of it isn't exactly safe."

Run now, Kit. Fucking run! This chick will ruin anything else you ever try to have with another... because no one will ever compare. I just fucking know it.

My lips part, and I take in a breath, willing myself to walk the fuck away right now, but instead, I find my fucking voice.

"Well, if you must know... I imagine pushing my cock to the back of her throat, so rough and forceful that she gags. I want to hear that gargling noise. You know, the one when she's choking and gagging and saliva is spilling from her lips around my cock..." I reach up, extending my arm to wrap my hand around her throat, and those perfect plump lips part, a faint breath of air rushing out.

"And when I grip her neck," I continue, giving it a gentle squeeze. "I can feel my fucking cock thrust in and out of the column of her throat. I can feel her struggle to breathe, but I can't let up because it feels soooo fucking good, and all I want to do is make her choke. Make her hurt until my cum shoots straight down her oesophagus into her stomach."

I expect Bell to cringe. To screw her face up and tell me I'm disgusting, but as usual, she simply wears a look of indifference as she leans into my hand gripping her throat.

"Are you hoping she'll vomit from the gagging?" she asks, and fuck, I don't know how she says the words without a single fucking emotion on her face.

"No, I'm not into puke play. I just want to feel the gag. The tightening of her throat as her body coils tight from the reflex."

"And the choking." She reaches up, resting her hand over mine, and urging me to grip her neck tighter. "Are you hoping to cut off her air? Make her pass out?"

"I don't want to kill her if that's what you're asking?"

She shakes her head. "Nope, not asking that. But you want to restrict her air, right? Dominate her so much that you control the oxygen she gets? Push her to the brink of possible death, where she could even pass out from the lack of oxygen?"

"Yes," I admit quickly, sure she'll bolt any second, but instead, she nods, dropping her hand from mine, her fingers moving to the buttons on the front of her dress.

Wait... is she... undoing them?

"Good. You'll do," she murmurs, bobbing her head down at my pelvis. "Get it out then."

I'm almost positive I will regret this later, and not at all because I'm about to get choked on my best friend's brother's cock. But because, I'm not sure if Kit really has what it takes to follow through with something he's only ever imagined doing.

"You really want to do this after what I just admitted?" he asks, even while he slips off his tank.

"Yes."

"Are you sure?" he asks again, his voice dropping an octave as I part the front of my dress, giving him a glimpse of my black lacy bra.

"Do we have to go over this again, Kitty Kat? Do I ever lie?"

His brows shoot up. "Fine. It's your funeral."

"In that case..." I peer up at him through the fan of my lashes. "Since you have a Santa Dom kink, why don't you go and slip on that Santa costume hanging in your wardrobe. May as well get right into the role of it."

His lips part in shock, and it takes him a moment to clear his throat enough to speak.

"You saw the suit?"

I nod. "I might have snooped in there first," I admit, standing from the bed and letting my dress slip off my shoulders to pool at my feet.

His eyes are searing as they peruse down, taking in every part of exposed skin he can see.

"I wear it so the security cameras pick up Santa in the feed, and I show Libi..." he trails off, clearly distracted by my near nakedness.

Snapping my fingers before his eyes, he flinches back, and a low growl rumbles in his chest like he wants nothing more than to shove me down and fuck me raw right here, right now, and hell... I want to let him.

"Santa suit," I order, and he grins this time, turning and walking into the room that is set up like a fancy designer store dressing room. Only this one isn't in a store. It's right here in his home.

Sitting back on the bed, I unlace my boots and kick them off to the side, before standing and checking myself over in the ceiling to floor mirrors.

The red in my tattoo stands out especially well in this light, and the black looks darker. More sinister.

I love my ink. Pretty isn't a word I use to associate with myself, but since getting it done, and covering up all the scars, I really do feel pretty.

After getting my ink I started to dress differently. No more clothes right up to my neck. No more lacy long sleeves to hide the deliberate imperfections. Some done by me. Others done by my father.

In certain light, if someone is looking closely enough, I know they can see indents from some of the cigarette burns in my skin, but mostly they go unnoticed until someone tries to touch me where the tattoos are.

"Please tell me I don't have to wear the fucking beard too. It's too fucking hot for that shit."

My eyes flick to Kit's reflection in the mirror as he comes to stand behind me, the thin red pants hanging low on his hips, the cheap fabric not doing anything to hide the bulge underneath. The red jacket is more like a shirt, which he's left open with the sleeves rolled up, revealing those rippling abs again, and the hat is nowhere in sight.

"Is it bad that I want to get a knife and mark-up those washboard abs?" I ask, and his brows hitch, but he doesn't panic like most guys would.

"Is it bad that I'd let you, as long as you promised to lick up the blood?"

My lips part as air whooshes from me, and I spin to face him as heat pools between my legs.

Shit. I'm *feeling*… like *actually* feeling.

I'm hot, yet goosebumps ripple over my skin. My blood is molten, rushing through my veins to get to my pussy. My heart is thudding in my chest like a drum, so loud I can hear it in my ears. And there's something else. Something that feels like more than arousal, yet I can't place it, because I've never felt it before.

My chest is rising and falling so quickly that he notices, his eyes jumping to the way my tits strain towards him like they are desperate for his touch.

"You like the sound of that? Licking up my blood?" His blue gaze flicks back to lock with mine.

"Yes," I breathe, and he steps closer, his hand reaching out, and a second later, he's fisting my hair, jerking my head back.

"Tell me again how rough you like it."

"As rough as you can handle, and probably more." I pant as he hovers over me, his lips mere inches from mine.

"Open your mouth," he demands, and yes, his dominance has me melting, my lips parting for him instantly.

"Tongue out," he snaps, and I do it, making sure to stretch it as I go, curling the tip so it's more inviting.

Then he spits on my tongue.

A moan escapes me, his warm spit slapping my tongue, and I drag it in and swallow it down, accepting his filthy gift.

"Mmmm. You taste good, Santa."

With slightly parted lips, a slow, sinister smile spreads them wide.

"Are you a filthy whore, Belladonna?"

"Only for those who deserve it, Kitty Kat."

He growls at the name I call him, but, fuck it, he deserved that dig after calling me Belladonna.

"You're meant to call me Santa," he snaps, and like the brat I am, I roll my eyes.

"I'd call you Santa every fucking time if you deserved it. But you're being a shit-cunt, calling me the very thing you know hurts."

His eyes narrow. "I thought you liked pain."

"Not *that* pain."

For a long moment, he stares into my eyes, his blue orbs dancing between mine like he's trying to see the depravity behind them.

"No. I guess that's not the sort of pain we should share," he rasps, his fist gripping my hair painfully tight as he reaches around with his free hand and unclips my bra.

The moment my tits spill free, he lets up on his grip, shifting back to get a good ganda at my rack, and I keep my eyes trained on his, so I don't miss the surprise when it happens.

Ohhh, there it is.

"Nipple piercings." He groans. "Fuck, Bell. I should've known."

"If you make me pass out from choking me on your cock,

I might let you hook a battery up to them and give me a little zap."

His eyes flare as they lock back with mine. "You're into erotic electrostimulation?"

This time it's my brows that shoot up in surprise. "You know what that is? Not many do."

His grin reappears. "Fuck, I hope my sister doesn't come home for days. The things I want to do to you…"

"Yes," I moan.

"Yes, to what?" he rasps, leaning in close. So close I can feel the warmth of his breath fan over my lips.

"Yes, to anything you want to do."

"Fuck," he rushes out, and a second later, his lips are on mine.

I melt into him, letting his tongue sweep into my mouth as I try to keep up, not used to kissing anyone.

Shit. Suddenly, I feel out of my depth.

You can string me up like a pig. Whip me like a slave. Fuck me with weird objects. But kiss me… hell, I don't even know how to do that confidently.

It takes me a few beats to relax as he slows the kiss, like he can feel my uneasiness, and he slowly grazes his tongue with mine a few times before I feel game enough to delve mine into his mouth.

When I do, I feel his moan vibrate in his chest more than I can hear it. So I do it again, and his fingers dig into my hips before he breaks the kiss.

"Fuck, Bell," he pants, licking his lips as I do the same. "We'll talk about that kiss later, but right now, I need you to get on your fucking knees."

My eyes flare at his demand, and with our gazes locked, I drop to my knees before him.

"You look so fucking good down there. Kneeling for me like you're begging for my cock."

"I don't beg," I murmur before reaching out and tugging on the red fabric of his pants, revealing more of that delicious V on his lower abdomen. "But I will choke for you."

His top lip curls, almost like he hates me, and hell if that doesn't make me want him even more. I shouldn't want this. Want him. He's ten years older and my best friend's brother, but I can't deny my body when it feels this in tune with another.

"Open wide, Bell," he rasps, shoving the red pants all the way down to pool at his ankles, giving me the first glimpse of his long hard cock.

And long it is, curling at the end in a way that I know will reach the hard to get A-spot deep inside me. But what's even more exciting about this bendy beast is the fact that it might actually make me gag.

I haven't told him that I don't really have much of a gag reflex. I don't know why that is, and it makes me a good deep throater, but that bend is going to press on parts that normally get missed.

Peering up at him, I try to look as innocent as I can, knowing guys like that shit.

"Don't forget, do it exactly the way you imagine when you're fucking that toy," I remind him. "Hard. Rough. Brutal. And most of all, unrelenting."

His nostrils flare as he fists my hair again. "Pinch my leg if you need me to stop."

"I won't," I smirk and part my mouth wide, sticking my tongue out just in time for him to press his hard tip to it.

Then he surges all the way in, right to the back of my throat.

His invasion, the hiss that falls from his lips, and the way his pupils are blown has me instantly high.

He starts thrusting, not even giving me a moment to get used to his size, his dominant confidence has my body responding. My panties are already soaked. Sweat dots my skin. There's fire in my veins. And just like I'd hoped, his bendy cock has my body reacting with a gurgled gag.

"Fuck yes," he growls, releasing my hair and grabbing something off the bed next to us.

A moment later, he hooks my bra around the back of my head, using it to control me.

"Give me more of that filthy sound, Bell. Show me how your body tries to repel me."

His words are like a spark, because the gargle returns as his tip hits deep down my throat, my body coiling tight, my throat closing around his shaft.

"Yes. Take it. Choke on it." He thrusts over and over, holding my head in place with my bra.

Tears stream from my eyes, and I'm glad I don't have waterproof eyeliner on today, so he can see the evidence of the mess he's made of me when he's done.

He's relentless, just as I'd hoped, his hard cock girthy enough to make my jaw ache. The only time he eases up, is when I actually nearly puke, but even then, he keeps his cock in my throat as I work to breathe through my nose, trying to go for as long as I can so he can get over the line.

Letting go of the bra, his thrusts slow as he grips the top of my head with one hand, and the column of my throat with the other, sending a rushing thrill through me.

Yes. This. He's going to make me suffer.

"Fuck, Bell. I can feel my cock. It's so far in." He pants as our eyes meet again, his hand massaging the column of my throat as he feels his length fill it. "Look at you, all fucking messy for me. You look perfect like this."

I know what's coming next, given the way he's holding my head, and I beg him with my eyes to do it.

Please... just do it. Make me pay. Make me choke. I'm at your mercy. Do whatever you want to me.

When his eyes flare, I wonder if he can read my thoughts because he thrusts hard once, twice, and on the third time, he holds my face to the base of his shaft as he hits all the way in, choking me, gagging me, and suffocating me with my nose buried against the base of his pelvis.

I can't breathe, and my reflexes kick in, trying to fight. Trying to force me to pull away to get the air I need. To stop my body's violent heaves. I jerk, gargling, trying to gasp for air, but I already know none can get in.

I gag, and watery saliva comes straight up, right before he releases my head and pulls all the way out.

Gasping for air, I nearly tumble forward against his thighs as I start coughing and choking on the pooled saliva and drool coming from my mouth. It coats my chest, drizzling down into my navel, some soaking into the top of my panties.

"You're such a dirty girl." Kit pants. "I should've used and abused this body years ago."

I nod, not able to speak for a moment as I catch my breath, and the moment I do, I grin up at him with a wicked glint in my eyes.

"This time, hold my nose and don't pull out," I say hoarsely, my voice raspy from the abuse. "The moment you start to feel me fade, I'd better feel you cuming down my throat or I'll bite your dick off."

A laugh bursts from his lips. "You know you'll pass out, right?"

"Exactly." I nod, and he nods in return, no longer surprised by my bedroom antics.

"Time to suffocate on my cock then, like a good fucking whore."

Have I imagined my sister's Satan worshipping best friend on her knees like this before?

Fuck yes. Hard not to when she always spoke about sex like she's discussing the fucking weather.

I never told anyone though. Not my mates. Not the guys from my platoon. Not even Wes... and fuck, we've swapped more truths than most men survive.

Now she's here on her knees. Black smears running from her eyes to leave a dirty trail down her cheeks. Those lips that she used to hide behind black lipstick, fuck, they are the perfect shade of pink, all swollen and rolled back as she takes my cock into her mouth like a fucking pro.

Fuck. Maybe she is. Maybe this is exactly what she does for a living.

I used to tag her as the enemy. Still kinda do. Most women fall into that category by default with me. But I'm working on that.

My hangups aren't great. It's fucking wrong that every woman I look at besides my sister and daughter has me throwing walls up. But fuck, I go to therapy when I can... sometimes.

Therapy is fucking draining. I know where it all stems from. My cunt of a mother.

She traded me for her next high, giving me to sick foul women that liked to abuse. I learned really fucking quick that women could wound deeper than the bullets I've dug from my flesh. It's taken years to scrub those fucking lessons from my brain, but some days, the stain of them fucking shows through.

Bell Bishop though... she never fit that pattern. She carries her own wounds. She's experienced another kind of evil, and despite that, she holds her head high and faces this fucked up world like a fucking warrior.

I used to hate that about her. Jealous I couldn't be the same.

I've kept my distance because the more I hated her, the more I wanted her.

Fuck. I've been obsessed from day one.

Intrigued. In awe. Completely fucking infatuated.

I even thought I was in love with her right before I married Rhonda.

She's chaos in combat boots, and I've been tracking her in the shadows for years.

So why am I crossing the line now?

"Kill me with your cock."

Fuuuuck, that's why.

She stretches her lips wide, those big dark eyes locking with mine as she gives me a command and consent in one breath.

Every muscle locks up as I fight the trained soldier in me to stand the fuck down.

Take the fucking shot, Kit. She's giving herself to you on a fucking platter.

Control is something I've mastered. Drilled into me through therapy and combat training. I need to measure the response. Tame the fucking rage and keep it leashed.

So what the fuck is this?

Violence.

That's what I feel when I fuck. That's what I feel now.

But with her, the line blurs. She's not afraid of the part of me I fight to bury. She's calling it out. Daring me to trust it.

"Shift back," I order, my voice low and deep as I point to the bed.

She moves without hesitation, her body language fluent as she shifts and leans her back against the side of my mattress. Her dark eyes lock with mine as she rests her head back, her lips open wide like she's desperate to taste my cock.

Fuck, she's stunning. A dark beauty. Probably the hottest thing I've ever seen with those plump tits more than a firm handful, her nipples such a deep rose colour, peaked hard with silver barbell piercings... I frown as I lean closer, getting a better look at those fucking piercings.

"Fuck, Bell. Are those skulls?" I take in the silver diamond encrusted skull heads at each end of the barbell, and when I glance up, she nods, her red-tipped fingers coming up to pinch each nipple.

She doesn't speak, her mouth still wide, reminding me of one of those cheap-ass blow up dolls.

Reaching down, I bat her hands away and roll each nipple between my fingers, my gaze tracking how her eyes roll in the back of her head momentarily.

Fuck. The fact that she's so turned on by me, the guy she hates with a passion... well, fuck. I'm gonna make this brutal.

The violence inside me shifts, still lurking at the surface but no longer wrapped in hate.

It's a violent sort of hunger and need. I don't just *want* to take, but fuck, I want to *give*.

And fuck, I'll give it all to her.

She wants my violence. She craves it.

A low growl rumbles in my chest as I release her nipples, and fist my cock, watching her eyes flare with desire.

"This what you want?" I snarl through gritted teeth, feeling the violence build inside me like a fucking rush, and fuck... she nods.

"You want my cock, Bell? You want to fucking choke on it?"

She nods again, her reaction triggering every instinct I've spent years containing.

I slap my hard rod across her cheek, and her nostrils flare, her hands whipping up to wrap around the backs of my thighs, urging me forward.

Another savage growl falls from me as I steer my cock to her lips and forcefully surge in.

She stiffens even as she holds my legs in place like she wants more, and I widen my stance, making sure I get the right angle to penetrate her throat all the way down, my hand fisting her hair again to hold her to me with each deep thrust.

She gags, and my cock fucking swells as her throat constricts around me.

"Fuck... yes... take it. Fucking take it." I snarl, curling my lip as I let my rage rush to the surface.

I fuck into her mouth and throat relentlessly, revelling in the power I hold right now, yet a part of me knows I should be concerned with how much she likes being abused like this.

Fuck, I'm concerned at how much I love doing it.

But shit, she doesn't pinch me, just holds me closer, even forcing her head forward as much as she can as I seat myself right to the hilt.

Her body is fighting, even though her mind isn't. It's a natural reflex to want to fight the intrusion, and the gagging grows more intense as I fuck her throat with strong punches.

"Fuck, you're such a slut, Bell," I seethe, going faster, and her lids flutter closed like she's getting fucking high. "Open your eyes!" I demand. "I wanna see those tears as you fade."

Her lids snap open with a flare, and I can feel her weakening under each punch of my hips, her grip on my legs lightening.

"Fuck. Yes. Fuck. Take it." I roar. "Fucking take it!"

As pleasure rushes to my nuts, I do as she asked before, pinching her nose, cutting off all of her air, and she convulses around me as her body protests, and fuuuuck, I can't hold back any longer, my climax hitting me like a fucking sledgehammer as I start shooting cum right down her throat.

She shudders as I watch her, and fuck... did she just come too? I can't fucking tell as I watch her fade quickly, her eyes rolling into the back of her head and I pump more and more into her before her body finally goes limp.

"Fuuuuck. You were made for me," I rasp, knowing she's out cold and can't hear that fucking admission.

Easing my cock from her abused mouth, her head lulls to the side, so I give her face a little tap.

"Bell. Wakey, wakey."

Nothing.

"Bell..." I slap her face harder.

Still nothing.

"Bell!" I yell, shaking her, and her fucking head lulls forward.

Fuck! Fuck! Fuck!

I fucking killed her!

"No, Bell! Fuck!"

I drag her flat to the floor, pressing my fingers to her neck to check for a pulse.

"Fucking hell. Don't you die on me!" I find a faint thrum of her pulse, and as relieved as I am to feel it, it's fucking weak.

Rolling her onto her side in the recovery position, I force

my fingers into her mouth, scooping out the residual cum, before thumping her back a few times.

Looking up, I spot my phone sitting on the far bedside table.

Fuck. I need to call an ambulance.

A choked gagging sound lurches from Bell, and her entire body coils as she starts coughing up some of my cum that must have been deep down in her throat.

I rub her back as my panic fades, but my fear still remains, because shit... I nearly killed her. I let go for the first time with another person, and I fucking nearly killed her.

Bell hacks up some more, pushing herself up on her elbow, and once she's done, she flops back on the floor, her gaze trained on the ceiling as her lips spread wide in a grin, and fuck, her pupils are blown like she's high.

Shit, is she?

"Have you taken something?" I snarl, and with that lazy smirk, she lolls her head from side to side.

"No, Kitty Kat. You're the only thing that's made me high." Her lazy stare flicks to me. "Don't worry."

My brows shoot up. "Don't worry?"

"Nine hundred and nineteen days, remember?" She slurs. "I'm not throwing that away for anything."

I fucking gape at her. "I nearly killed you."

She shrugs, panting. "I'm still alive. Relax."

"Relax?" I fucking squeak like my voice just broke. "Bell... what I did—"

Her hand slaps haphazardly over my mouth. "Shhhh. Your concern is too loud." She drops her hand to the carpet, patting it. "Come down here with me."

I realise I'm fucking heaving, so I work to calm my breathing and slow my racing heart, shuffling to lay down on the floor next to her.

For a few minutes, we lay there staring up at my ceiling in

silence. What we just did plays like a reel through my head, giving me snapshots of moments.

When I was doing that... fucking her throat with such brutality, I felt so fucking high. So powerful. I fucking loved hurting her like that, and it only confirms what I've suspected for a long time.

I'm a fucking sadist.

"Are you alright?" I rasp, breaking the silence.

"I'm amazing." She practically purrs, and in my periphery, I see her turn her head my way, so I do the same, locking eyes with her.

Fuck... what a sight she is.

"You're fucking beautiful like this." I prop myself up on my elbow, staring down at her as I trail my finger over the ink on her décolletage, tracing the scars underneath.

She stiffens a little, but doesn't stop me, so I lower my head and dart my tongue out, tasting the salt on her skin as I lick over a few of the raised imperfections.

But fuck. They are perfect to me.

"Kit," she whispers. "What are you doing?"

Lifting my head, I find her eyes and the flash of uncertainty in them.

"I'm enjoying your body," I say even as I glide my fingers down to her pebbled nipple and tug on the piercing.

Her lips part as a faint breath escapes her, so I shift down and wrap my lips over it, sucking her into my mouth as my tongue swirls over the peak and the skull heads on the barbell.

Bell's back arches as she moans, her hand fisting in my hair, holding me to her chest.

"I'm confused," she breathes, so I pop her nipple free and raise a questioning brow.

"About what?"

"I gave you what you wanted. Something you'd only ever dreamed of doing, and now you're..." she trails off, frowning.

"You gave me one thing, but we haven't fucked yet, so we are nowhere near done, Belladonna."

Her fist tightens in my hair painfully as she curls her lip. "Call me that again, and we are done here."

"You called me Kitty Kat before," I snap.

"It's a fucking pet name, Kit. I don't use the name of the thing you used to kill your parents."

She has a point, and while I normally like getting a rise out of her, I don't really want to hurt her emotionally.

"Apologies, Bellicent. I promise not to call you that again."

Her eyes narrow. "I haven't given you permission to call me that either."

I scoff, pinching her nipple between my fingers until she hisses from the pain. "I don't need permission to call you by your real name. Especially when you are in *my* bedroom."

Her hand loosens in my hair, and her gaze drops. "No one calls me Bellicent."

"That's because no one knows your real name. Well... besides my sister."

"We don't have to do this." She waves a hand between us.

"What? Talk?"

She nods. "Yeah."

My eyes narrow as I sit up. "Why the fuck not?"

She props herself up on her elbows. "Well... we're here to fuck, not talk."

"So, you don't ever talk to the guys you fuck?" I ask, and she scrunches her nose.

"God no. That would be weird."

"Why the fuck would it be weird?" I snap, and she gives me that familiar deadpan expression she does so well.

"Kit, I don't know what planet you come from, but in my world, I'm the girl guys want to fuck, not the girl guys want to keep. No conversation is needed. We each get what we want and move on. Don't make it weird."

For a long moment, I can't even fucking speak. Not because I'm feeling any sort of rejection by her wanting to fuck and flee, but by how fucking sad her words are.

She's the girl they want to fuck, but don't want to keep... is she seriously okay with that?

"What fuckheads do you let near this body, Bell? Because anyone who only wants a slice and then fucks off needs their fucking balls removed from their body."

Her lips quirk. "That's a bit violent."

"I'm a sadist, so it's not violent to me."

Her smile falls as she speaks quietly. "You really are a sadist, aren't you?"

My eyes drop to her tits as I shrug. "I had my suspicions."

She sits up abruptly. "Did I just help you have your awakening?"

"Shut up." I scoff, biting back my smirk, and fuck, her lips spread into a satisfied smile.

Shit, she has so many smiles for me today.

"Well, I'm a masochist, so this works." She points between us, and fuck, my heart starts to race.

I fucking know she's referring to sex, but I can't deny to myself that I want her to mean more than that.

I guess the obsession never died.

"You ever suffocated anyone by riding their face?" I ask out of the blue, and her brows shoot high as she slowly nods.

Fuck... could it be possible that she'd be into all the things I am?

"How about piss play?" I ask. "You into that?"

"If the piss doesn't taste like ass, then yeah." She shrugs nonchalantly.

"Back door?" I push for more, and she nods.

"Absolutely. You?"

Fuck. She's good. Not the least bit embarrassed about this conversation.

"I'd rather not be pegged." I shrug. "But I don't mind a chunky butt plug."

She smirks. "Noted. I don't mind my arse getting wrecked occasionally. Just give me a heads up so I can douche first. Otherwise, it'll get messy."

My fucking heart flips in my chest.

"I told you..." I smirk. "I like messy."

She rolls her eyes. "Well, consider *that* sort of mess a hard limit for me... if we can help it."

"Noted." I grin. "I wanna fuck you bare."

At my admission, she freezes, her brows high and her expression flickering with concern.

"Bare?"

"Yes. No barrier," I tell her, my cock already weeping at the thought of sinking inside her and feeling the real flesh of her walls.

"How often do you do that?" she asks.

"Never. Well... only once. Which resulted in Libi," I admit, and her shoulders relax a little.

"Then why do you want to do that with me?"

Shit. She wants my honesty, something I can never usually give to women, but with her, right now... well it just feels different.

"Because you said you'll let me do all the things I imagine but can't do with other women. So I wanna do that. I wanna feel every fucking inch of you, flesh to flesh."

"Okay," she agrees quickly. Breathily.

"Yeah?" I walk my hands up the carpet on each side of her body, forcing her to lay back.

"Now?" she asks as she stares up at me, but I shake my head.

"Nope. Now, I wanna see how many of my fingers you can

take." I follow this by trailing my hand down over her thin waist, moving to her mound.

"What if I told you I can take your whole hand?"

My digits still just over her slit as my eyes widen.

"Can you?"

She shrugs. "Don't know. I've never been fisted before but I bet it would hurt." A slow, sinister smirk stretches her lips wide.

"Fuck, Bell." My cock jerks and my heart nearly thumps through the wall of my chest. "Would you let me hurt you like that?"

"Please." She moans. "Make me hurt good."

7

―――――

BELL

His fingers instantly ignite heat deep in my core as he circles my clit, and even though all my blood is rushing to that area, I can't focus on anything but the way he's looking at me.

Usually, the guys I fuck like to watch what their fingers are doing, not the expression on my face. But not Kit. His eyes roam my face as his digits work over my nub, his gaze tracing my lips, nose, cheeks and when he connects with my eyes, I swear he's trying to see right into my thoughts.

Maybe he's checking if I have a soul. Too bad, he's shit out of luck there.

"Should I start slow?" he asks, moving his fingers from my clit to delve gently through my slick folds.

"No need. I'm ready." I pant as the pads of his fingers tease my entrance.

"Yeah?" he asks, still bloody watching my face. "How many fingers are you ready for?"

He follows that by easing three in, and my back arches as my lips part, my moan loud in the quiet room.

"Fuuuuck, your cunt is so hot and slick, Bell. I can't wait to sink my cock in there."

"Uh-ha," I agree breathily, my chest rising and falling quickly as he starts fucking me with his fingers.

"But first, I wanna see what it feels like to sink my whole fist in there," he growls, quickly slipping a fourth finger in, and I cry out at the slight sting, my lips spreading into a smirk as he gives me what I'm craving.

Pain.

"Fuck, the way you just gushed over my hand." He leans down with another animalistic growl and snatches my bottom lip between his teeth, biting until I cry out.

He releases my lip with a long drag of his teeth, chuckling darkly. "Every time I make you hurt, your cunt gets slicker."

"I guess you know you're doing the job right then," I rush out, pushing my pussy against his hand with each thrust, feeling his fingers deep, while his thumb grazes my clit.

"Fuck, Bell. Give me a safeword."

"I don't need it." I pant, my lids falling shut as his rhythm makes it hard to be uncomfortable with his studying gaze.

"Like fuck. Safety first, Bell. Always."

Fuck it. Why does he have to be so… decent?

I don't do safewords, and yeah, I know that's dangerous as fuck, but that's the point.

Do I have a death wish?

Maybe. But if I really think about it, the rush of being humiliated, being pushed to the brink and then over, the possibility that this is it… well, it's just another kind of addiction.

I don't need drugs and alcohol when I'm walking that fine line between living and dying.

I've been diagnosed as having borderline sexual masochism disorder, and that paired with what we did before, a form of asphyxiophilia, is seriously dangerous. So, to me, a safeword isn't needed.

"Since I don't do the whole con non-con thing," I pant,

thrusting up to meet his rhythm, "if I say no or stop, then those words mean no or stop."

"Noted," he growls, before claiming my lips.

I'm stunned for a moment, still not used to this whole kissing thing during sex, but the moment his tongue sweeps against mine, I melt, and something happens...

I get lost in the kiss.

His fingers, his thumb, the feel of his soft lips against mine, his tongue brushing mine and fucking into my mouth... shit... this is a different sort of high.

I'm about to push him back, because I don't know if I like this feeling, but he beats me to it, breaking the kiss with a hiss as he fucks his fingers into me harder.

"Does this hurt?"

"A little. Not enough," I admit, and holy fuck, the wicked smirk that tugs at his lips is seriously sinful.

"Time to take my fist then."

My lips part as a breath rushes from me, and he shifts lower, settling between my legs as his eyes finally focus on my pussy.

"Your clit is so swollen," he rasps, leaning down to suck it into his mouth.

My back arches as I cry out, white hot heat flushing through my entire body, and he moans, like he loves the taste of me, the vibration of it adding to the sensations.

Kit draws back, sucking my clit and stretching it until it pops free, and his eyes lock with mine as he licks his lips.

"I'm gonna love destroying this pussy."

A slow smirk pulls at my lips at how much I want that. "Get to it then."

His smirk is lazy, but the flare of his eyes as they drop to watch his fingers fuck in and out of me is full of anticipation.

Reaching behind him with his free hand, he rifles through

his partially open bedside drawer and brings out a bottle of lube, smirking as he holds it up high, flicks the cap open, and starts pouring it all over his hand, and my pussy.

For a flicker of a moment, I'm worried about the carpet underneath me, but he doesn't seem concerned. His only thought right now is hurting me, and fuck if that doesn't make me even hotter for him.

Easing his fingers out of me, he lathers them up too, slathering more all over my folds before sinking the four fingers right in again. I moan and arch and melt at the sting of pain, and when our eyes meet, I know he's ready to make me hurt so fucking good.

"When you start to feel too tense, rub that pretty clit for me so I can focus on spreading you impossibly wide, okay?"

I nod, biting my lip as a thrill rushes through me.

I want this.

I want him to force his hand inside me.

I want it to hurt.

And I want it to consume me.

"Here we go," he murmurs, his eyes now focused between my legs as his fingers ease out a little, and he adds his thumb.

The pain is biting at my entrance, stretching me, the thinner part of my opening near my perineum stinging, and I know I'll feel that pain for a few days. But fuck, who cares, because it's making me melt even more.

"Fuck yes, Bell. You get so much slicker when I hurt you." Kit hisses like he's struggling to stay in control. "Do you need pain to come?"

"Sometimes," I admit, trying to part my legs wider, desperate for his hand to breach.

"Do you need it now? Tonight?"

"Yes," I pant. "Please."

"Fuck, okay." His hand moves from side to side, twisting

to work inside me, the pain flaring hot between my legs as he tries to force his hand past my resistance.

"What about objects?" he asks, his eyes flicking up to meet mine as he works his hand in a fraction more. "Do you like to be fucked with objects?"

"Yeah. Anything really." I breathe, "especially if it's big or has rough edges so it hurts."

"Fuck. You have no idea how much you're turning me on right now," he growls, his gaze focused on his hand and trying to feed it inside me. "What things have you fucked before?"

His words, the images they are putting in my head, are making me slicker, and I realise he's doing it on purpose.

"The usual. Cucumbers, carrots, a hairbrush handle, a can of deodorant, a TV remote..." My words come out strangled as more pain flares between my legs. It's not just the stretch of my lips, but the pressure of his hand trying to force in past my tense muscles.

Remembering what he said before, I quickly press my fingers to my clit, while my other hand focuses on my nipple, and try to help release some of the tension.

"I tried a bed knob once..." I pant. "Couldn't get it in... was frustrating."

He chuckles. "I bet it was. I can see how much you want to be completely filled." He squirts more lube over our connection. "I'm confident I can do this, but it will hurt, Bell. I'll have to force my way in."

I moan at his words, my eyes locking with his. "Don't act like that isn't turning you on, Kit. If you want to hurt me, then fucking do it."

A deep growl falls from his lips as they curl, and fuck, Satan, please take my soul because he looks like he wants to maim.

"Come on then, open up," he snarls. "Be a good fucking girl and let me in."

With a savage and brutal shove, I scream and stiffen, my back arching as he forces his way in, past my resistance, and I mash my fingers over my clit, while pulling hard on my nipple, and just like that, I detonate.

With each crashing wave of my climax, I suck his hand in deeper, and I can see his lips moving, but I can't hear anything but the rush of my pulse like a fucking hammer in my ears as white light rims my vision.

He's on his knees, one hand fully buried inside me while his other is pumping his cock as ropes of cum shoot from his tip, all over my hand, clit, and impossibly stretched pussy.

As my orgasm fades, my hearing returns, our panting breaths loud in his room.

"Fuck, look how good you take my whole hand." His voice is rough as he gives his cock one last pump. "You fucking swallowed my fist, Bellicent. I can feel everything inside you."

Jesus Christ. I fucking gush again at his words, and he chuckles, feeling it.

How is that even possible? I literally just came.

"I fucking love seeing my whole fist disappearing inside you," he growls, and I push up on my elbows, still in pain but wanting to see too.

I'm panting, more arousal building in me as the pain of his fist easing out a little and then sinking back in, sets me on fire again.

"Look, you can see me moving inside you," he rasps, twisting his hand, and ohhhh, just above my pubic bone, I can see my skin rolling with the motion of his hand. "Shit, you're gushing again."

My eyes dart to his, and for a long moment, we both stare at each other.

I don't recognise this feeling I keep getting. It's weird, yet warm. Like a heated blanket on a cold day. But also thrilling, like I'm on the precipice of something new. Something Bell Bishop has never experienced before.

"I don't freak you out?" I ask, my voice husky, yet strangely lacking my usual confidence.

Kit frowns at my question, sitting there between my legs with his fist literally buried inside me. "Do I freak you out?"

I shake my head.

"Then why would you think you freak me out?"

"I hate to state the obvious, Kitson, but I'm not exactly normal. Most guys want to have a ride on the freak train, but bolt quickly afterwards, fucking terrified of me and the things I enjoy."

Shifting, Kit leans forward until our noses are mere inches apart, and with his free hand, the one that isn't deep in my cunt, he fists my hair and tugs me forward until we are breathing the same air.

"They aren't terrified of you, Bell. They are terrified of how much they fucking like the stuff they experience with you, and that's on them, because they cave to society's norms. They are the men who visit kink clubs and only use cash so there's no evidence. They are the ones who are married, unhappily, who have vanilla sex with their wives, too scared to ever ask them to be a part of their fantasies." Kit jerks me closer, our lips brushing as he speaks. "They are the type of cowards that don't deserve a woman like you, Bellicent. They don't even deserve a fucking ride, let alone a second fucking thought."

His lips crash to mine and something snaps inside me, turning me almost feral as I kiss him back, biting at his lips, his tongue, and moaning when he does it back, digging his teeth into my lip so hard that I taste blood.

His hand starts moving inside me again, the pain of it amping up my pleasure, and despite how wrong I know it is to do this a second time tonight, I reach up, tugging on his wrist until he releases my hair, and I guide his hand to my throat, urging him to squeeze.

And he does. His fingers wrap around the column of my throat, putting pressure on the outside while avoiding too much pressure on my trachea, like he's done this before.

The rush of it builds quickly, feeling the biting pain of his hand stretching my pussy, the way his fingers punch into my cervix and dig deep into my hard to reach A-spot has heat and pain mingling in the best way, all while he deprives me of oxygen.

My head feels light and floaty, and I give myself over to him completely.

"Sharing?" His voice has my eyes snapping open as he fist fucks me. "You into that?"

I open my mouth to speak, but because I'm so lightheaded, my words are slurred.

"You want a… threesome?" I breathe out. "Let me guess… two chicks and you?"

He smirks wickedly, shaking his head as he leans in close.

"No actually. My mate and I… with *you*." He nips at my parted lips. "Would you be into that?"

He feels it before I can even answer with words. The way I grow slicker at the very idea of being shared between him and his mate has a deep chuckle rumbling in his chest.

Ignoring how my body has already answered him, I try to take in as much air as I can so I can speak, feeling the rush about to hit, and knowing I'm going to come and pass out any moment.

"I'm into it… as long as you don't care about sharing." I gasp for air, and he fists me faster, harder. "Men can get possessive… even when it's a casual hookup."

"You don't have to worry about that with me and Wes, Bell. Sharing is one thing we do fucking well. He's a sadomasochist. So together, the three of us will either fucking work," he punches into me quickly, and pain flares like wildfire, "or we'll kill each other."

And just like that, I come again, in a spasm of gripping waves that has me shuddering, even as I feel like I'm floating. I grin as black rims my vision and I feel myself slipping away, and the last thing I see is Kit Hall's euphoric face before darkness takes me.

8

KIT

The sight of Bell's swollen folds, red and glistening, swallowing my hand is something else. Fuck. I don't think I've ever been more turned on in my life. To see my hand vanish inside her completely, and for her to take me right to the wrist, even though I know it hurt.

Fuck.

Just… Fuuuuck!

Releasing her neck, I lean down and check that she's still fucking breathing before I ease my hand from deep inside her cunt. Even the fact that she so easily blacks out, knowing I could do anything to her while she's unconscious, has the blood thrumming through my veins.

Fuck, that thought has me grinning.

"I bet you like that idea, don't you, Bell? The fact I could do anything to you while you're like this and you can't do anything to stop me?" I wrap my cunt-soaked hand around my cock, giving it a tight slow pump.

Fuck, her cream looks good on me. I want more. So much more.

Shifting, I slip my arms under her, scooping her up off the carpet and laying her lax body across my bed.

She's at my mercy right now as I position her legs apart, giving me enough access to that sweet pussy.

"Fuck, Bellicent," I murmur quietly, taking in the sight of her completely naked on my bed, those fucking skull barbells in her nipples making my mouth water. "I think you were always meant to be mine."

She doesn't respond of course, still out cold, so with cock in hand, I kneel between her splayed legs, still wearing the red fucking Santa shirt, but not willing to take it off because... well, I do kinda have a Santa kink, which really is just another form of Daddy kink, wanting my little masochist to submit to me.

And fuck, she submits so good.

Shifting closer to heaven, I steer my cock towards her swollen entrance, running the fat head of it through her wet folds a couple of times, circling her inflamed clit, before going back to her opening and easing in.

I grit my teeth as her slick hot heat envelops my hard length, and it surprises me how fucking tight it is given my whole fucking fist was just up there.

Ahhh the female sex organs are a fucking miracle to be marvelled.

"Fuuuck, Bell..." I hiss through gritted teeth as she adjusts around me. "You feel so fucking good."

Good is an understatement. Aside from the drunken night I fucked up with cunt-face Rhonda, in all of my thirty years, my cock has never felt the inside of another woman's cunt without the barrier of a condom. Fuck... this is something else.

Hot silk. Molten fucking heaven, that's what it is.

I slowly ease my cock out and back in a few times, my gaze darting from where we are joined, back to her face, her eyes still closed, expression still neutral.

"I bet you love the idea of waking up and finding me fucking you," I thrust faster, harder. "Don't you?"

Fuck, the sight of her body jostling with my thrusts, still completely slack, is a turn on of its own.

She's completely at my mercy. My little doll to do with as I please.

She's fucking perfect.

I fuck her harder, bringing my fingers to her clit to give the swollen nub some attention.

"Come on. Be a good girl and wake up for Santa," I growl, circling faster as I thrust.

Her chest rises and falls in a big breath, and I grin knowing she's slowly waking up.

"That's it. Rise and shine, Bell. Feel how Santa is fucking you."

A muffled moan falls from her plump lips as her head slowly lolls from side to side, so I piston harder, making her feel every fucking punch of my cock.

"Do you feel me, Bell?" I pant, fucking into her faster. "Do you feel how well I'm using your body as my fuck toy?"

"Kit," she breathes, her lids still closed, but fuck, I love the sound of my name falling from her lips. I love how completely she trusts me.

"Not Kit right now," I say roughly, my voice husky as the feeling of her cunt gripping me like a vice has every muscle in my body straining to stay in control. "Call me *Santa*."

Her eyes snap open, locking with mine as I loom over her, fucking into her tight heat, watching the way her tits jiggle with every brutal thrust.

"Say it!" I snarl, and a slow, lazy smirk spreads her lips wide.

I can't fucking tell if she's going to obey, or be a fucking brat, but fuck, both possibilities have my heart thrashing wildly in my chest.

"Santa," she purrs, her gaze turning mischievous. "Is that the best you can fuck me?" Then she fucking rears up and slaps me hard across the face.

My head whips to the side, and I still, my lip curling with a savage hiss as I turn back to face the fucking brat.

"It's like that, is it?" I snap, and she nods, wearing a shit-eating-grin, thoroughly satisfied with her little fucking love tap. "You wanna fight?"

She nods, her dark eyes bright as she takes me in, waiting eagerly like she wasn't just out cold moments ago.

"You want this to feel like non-con?" I ask, my fucking blood pumping hard through my body as I hope she fucking says yes.

In a flash, she rears up, getting in my face, her breath mingling with mine.

"I want to feel Santa fucking claim me."

Her words have barely left her lips before I fist the back of her hair, slamming my lips to hers brutally, feeling our teeth clash.

It's a biting, bruising kiss, with tongues and teeth, and fuck yes, blood. It could be hers or mine given how savagely our mouths battle, and a second later, I reef her head back by her hair, and spit in her gasping mouth.

"It's not just Santa who will be claiming you, Bellicent." I snarl, jerking her back even further so I can bend and snag her nipple and piercing between my teeth.

She cries out as I bite down hard, breaking the skin to taste more blood. I don't have to be concerned that she isn't fucking loving it, because her body tells me with a gush of slickness around my cock.

Releasing her nipple with a long sharp tug between my teeth, I jerk her head back to mine until we are nose to nose.

"I'll also be claiming you, Bell. And when that happens, I'm never fucking letting you go."

I thrust into her brutally as I release her head and shove her back, her body bouncing on my mattress.

As she claws at my chest in an attempt to fight me, I try to ignore the fucking fact I just told her I'm never letting her go.

I didn't mean to say that... did I?

"You can't claim me," Bell hisses, whipping her hand out to try to slap me again, and I lurch over her, trying to keep my cock buried inside her as we start fucking grappling.

"I fucking can," I grunt as she lands a hit, and my big palm engulfs her face, forcing it down onto the bed again as I hold it in place, fucking into her brutally. "You think the day I find someone that fucking matches me like this that I'm just letting them get away? Not a fucking chance, Bell."

"Fuck you!" she screams, although it's muffled by my hand as I smother her face with it while I pound into her.

"I am fucking you. This tight cunt is mine!" I practically yell, the force of my thrusts jolting her up the bed, further and further.

Bell's legs wrap around me, immediately halting my thrusts as her claw-like nails dig into my arm, drawing blood, and I finally release her face to see her fury.

"I am no one's!" she snarls, her nails whipping across my chest, and I suck in a breath before a deep growl rumbles from me.

"You want to play dirty, Bell? I can fucking play dirty!"

"Do it!" she hisses through her clenched teeth.

Fuck, she pushes me in the best fucking way, and I don't know why I didn't see this years ago.

I mean, I saw her. I always hated how much I thought about her and longed for something I probably shouldn't, given she's Tillie's best friend, but fuuuck, this side of her. How didn't I see it sooner?

She's my fucking match.

Reaching around my back, I grip her ankles, digging my

own nails into her skin and forcefully prying them loose, even as she slaps at my chest and face.

"Stop fucking slapping me!" I hiss, finally loosening her legs enough that I can force them back down to the mattress and hook my legs over them to pin her in place.

"Fuck you, Santa!" she snarls like a little savage, baring her teeth, her face still streaked with dry black tears.

She swings at me, this time with her fist, and I manage to intercept it just before it hits, both of us struggling against each other while my cock is still buried deep inside her, and harder than it's ever been.

"I will be the one fucking *you!*" I roar, wrangling her wrists into submission as I pin them to the bed.

We are both panting, but while she tries to struggle against my hold, I catch my breath and revel in the way our bodies line up so fucking perfectly.

"You can fight me all you want, Bell. Fuck, I don't even think you are role playing, but let me make one thing very fucking clear." I lean closer, feeling her panting breaths fan my lips. "The moment you trusted me to hurt you and use you, taking every fucking thing I did like it's something you've been craving your whole fucking life, was the moment you became mine. Love it. Hate it. I don't fucking care. Fight it all you fucking want." I start thrusting inside her again, and her lips part as the whisper of a moan escapes. "But it's happened, Bellicent Faith Bishop, and there's no going back now."

My cock punches into her savagely, and she cries out, her back arching off the bed as much as it can with me pinning her, and I thrust and thrust, over and over, brutally claiming her once and for all.

Her cunt is so fucking slick. There's no way her body isn't loving every minute of this, even if her brain is panicking with the reality of what this means.

Fuck. I don't even think I'm ready for what it means, but I give in to it, unleashing the part of me I keep locked away, not willing to show any other woman how fucking dark I can get.

"Do you hate me?" I snap, the wet noise of my cock slamming into her slick cunt filling the room.

"Yes!" she seethes, baring those fucking white teeth again. "I hate you so much!"

"Good fucking girl, Bell." I smirk and pant, feeling her walls grow tighter around me. "Because I fucking hate you too!"

She half screams, half snarls in fury, and I grit my teeth as she clamps around me, nearly ready to come.

"You feel my bare cock ripping you to shreds?" I pound hard, feeling my cock slam into her cervix, blow after blow.

"Yes," she cries, nearly there.

"I'm fucking you bare, Bell. No barrier. Just the skin of my cock buried in your slick cunt." I thrust harder, my nuts starting to fucking tighten. "I'm going to fill you up with my cum, Bell. Your cunt is going to be leaking for fucking days, and I'm not going to let you wash. I want you fucking filthy. Smelling of me and feeling your panties wet from me so you don't fucking forget who claimed this cunt!"

A scream rips from her as she starts coming, her walls kneading my cock in the best fucking way, and I know there's no way in hell I'll ever be able to fuck with a condom on again.

I can feel every hot, searing ripple of her cunt, the muscles hardening as her orgasm rolls through her, and before she's even finishing, I fucking let go, pleasure engulfing my core before the first jets of cum start shooting deep inside her.

"I'm filling you!" I roar, throwing my head back, and she ripples around me, sucking my cock in deep, like her pussy is desperate for my seed.

I can't remember the last time I came this hard, for so long, and with so much spilling from my body. It just solidifies that even though I didn't start this with the intention of claiming her, it's happened, and I'm okay with that.

As my muscles start to uncoil and my fucking hearing returns, I glance down at Bell to find her heaving from the intensity of her orgasm.

Fuck. She's beautiful, all dishevelled and messed up.

"Still hate me?" I pant, releasing her wrists and legs, part of me happy that this time, she didn't black out. She came hard, and felt every part of it, even the part where she comes down from her high.

"Always," she scoffs, and right as I ease out of her, the little brat slaps my face again.

My body aches under the hot spray of the shower, some places even stinging from the scratches marring parts of my skin. Bruises are already blooming, and probably the sorest parts of me are my lips and nipple, where the fucker bit me last night.

My pussy is a whole other story. She's swollen from the beating she took, and hell, it's the best feeling. I even love the burn I get from the slight tear when I pee.

I've been hiding in here way too long, anxious about seeing Kit after the things he said last night.

He claimed me. Like a barbarian. Like we live in a world where that's acceptable.

So why do I get stupid butterflies at the thought?

That's barbaric on its own, because this can't happen. Kit and I can never be a thing.

Hell, what we did has already crossed the line.

We fucked three times after the initial first time, and that was after a deep throat and a fisting session.

Hell's bells, did all of that really happen?

He's a fucking savage, and he matched me in every way.

Every time I went to get out of his bed, he wrestled me

back in and proved that he has the power to claim me all over again.

I tried to point out that just because he's physically stronger than me, doesn't mean he wins, but the guy is delulu, that's for sure.

I didn't mean to fall asleep in his bed. That's one thing I try to avoid when I hook up with guys, but one moment I was awake, having just come, and the next minute I was out like a light, only waking when the sun had risen and his side of the bed was empty.

I found my bag in the room at the foot of the bed. He must have fetched it while I was sleeping, although I don't know why. But I decided it was easier to shower in his bathroom instead of carting my stuff back down to the second floor with my thighs painted in his dry cum.

Shit. He really is a filthy fucker.

Who knew?

The smell of bacon has me hurrying, and I get out of the shower, drying off and dressing in another black summer dress, this one with little green skulls on it.

Grabbing my bag, I leave his room to go in search of the bacon... because... it's bacon, and I descend the first flight of stairs, wheeling my bag back into the guest room.

As I start down the second flight of stairs, my heart starts to race in my chest, and I rub at it feeling unusually nervous.

Shit... Bell Bishop doesn't get nervous. What the hell is going on?

Jesus fucking Christ. If Tillie was here right now, she'd read my betrayal all over my face.

I bet she'd hate me. Hate that I took my toxic traits and lured her big brother with them.

Shit, is that what I did? I can't even remember who made the first move. Everything after putting Libi to bed is a blur.

It has to be a post orgasm haze type of thing. Like

weaning off a bender or getting hit with a hangover after a big night of drinking.

Apparently, I have a Kit Hall hangover, and I'm not sure how to feel about it.

Downstairs, I find Kit in the kitchen, standing at the stove as he cooks, wearing only a pair of grey shorts, his top half completely bare.

Shit. His tanned skin and ink combination has my mouth watering to lick him.

Maybe I should go back upstairs, get my bags, and leave now.

"Libi!" Kit yells from the stove, his booming voice startling me, and he gasps at my gasp, spinning to face me.

"For fuck's sake, Bell. Stop fucking sneaking up on me."

I roll my eyes, thankful for his typical banter. "I didn't. You're just deaf because you're old."

A wicked grin crosses his face. "Oh yeah? Old didn't seem to bother you last night."

Shit. He has a point. Old really didn't bother me. In fact, old, or his version of old, was a goddamn blessing.

There's something to be said about experience.

His eyes flick over my shoulder to the staircase. "Libi! Breakfast!" he calls, and I cringe.

"Maybe she wants to sleep in."

For a long moment, he stares at me like I'm an idiot. "She's five. Never has she slept in and never does she take her time coming down for breakfast."

Well, don't I feel like an idiot.

"My bad. I'm not that familiar with the daily life of a five-year-old."

His expression softens. "Sorry. I'm not really a morning person."

I cringe. "That must suck when you have a kid."

He scoffs. "You have no idea."

Turning back to the stove, he turns off the burners, and I round the counter, taking a peek at what he's cooked up.

Yum. Bacon and scrambled eggs.

His eyes flick to me, and a smirk tugs at his lips as he starts to dish up the food. "You look well fucked."

Jesus, is it hot in here?

"You too," I say awkwardly, and holy hell, when have I ever been awkward?

"Thanks for grabbing my bag." I change the subject, clearing my throat. "I put it back in the guestroom."

He stills, his blue eyes snapping to mine. "Well, you can go and move it back into my room."

I scoff. "Unlikely."

Putting the pan down, he faces me fully, crossing his arms over his chest as he pins me with his glare.

"Was I unclear last night?" He growls, his brow pinching in the middle, clearly unhappy at this conversation.

Wait... was he serious last night?

"That was Santa," I point out, crossing my arms over my chest to match him. "We were playing."

Slowly, he shakes his head. "I *am* Santa, and we may have been playing, but I don't fucking make up shit like that."

Oh... Shit. He really was serious.

For a few long beats, we stare at each other, neither of us willing to break the battle of wills first, but I need to say something. This weird obsession with making me his has to stop.

"We can't do that," I say, studying every micro-shift in his expression.

"Why?" he snaps, and I roll my eyes, kinda figuring it was obvious.

"Tillie," I remind him, and he shakes his head.

"She will get over it." He drops his arms from his chest and turns back to finish serving us.

"I don't think you know your sister too well if you think she'll be alright with this," I snap, and he snaps right back.

"Why the fuck not? Why would she have a fucking problem with us?"

Is he serious? Does he not remember who he's talking to right now?

"She knows me, Kit. Too well."

"And?"

"And?" I throw my hands up and huff. "She knows my preferences, Kitty. I imagine she wouldn't want my emotional damage tainting you."

At the use of Kitty, he turns a hard glare my way, looking more lethal than I've seen him before.

Damn him. I like that look. I wonder if he'd hit me if I begged him to.

"Maybe you don't know my sister that well at all, Bell. She loves you. She'd never think of you like that."

"Have you forgotten where I came from? How I grew up? What I did to survive that?" I ask him, taking a step back as my anger rushes to the surface at even letting myself slightly remember my upbringing. "In my experience, even the most supportive people don't fully accept me, Kit. Tillie loves me. I know that. But facing this situation, I think you'll find that blood is thicker."

"You're fucking wrong." He tosses the tea towel down on the benchtop, taking a step towards me, but I take several back, making sure there's plenty of distance between us.

"I'd rather not risk my friendship and find out. Tillie is all I have. If I lose her, then I have no one, and as hard as it is to believe, I actually do need *someone*. I *need* her."

Just from his conflicted expression, I can tell there's a war battling inside his head, but he nods, stepping back to the bench.

"I'll talk to her."

I go to protest, but his bellow cuts me off.

"LIBI!"

"Kit, don't you dare say anything to her. I don't give you permission."

He scoffs. "I don't need your fucking permission, Bell."

I storm forward, fists balled. "The fuck you don't."

The moment I get close, he's on me, his hands engulfing each side of my face as he kisses me.

I try to fight it at first, but he's fucking stubborn, and unrelenting, and eventually, the combination of his spicy scent, the feel of his hard cock pressing against my pelvis, and the way his tongue tastes mine like he's fucking starved for me, has me melting.

Damn him. I kiss him right back even though I know I shouldn't.

When he breaks the kiss, we are both breathless, and his blue orbs look a little drunk as he stares at me. "Fight me in the bedroom all you like, Bell. But don't fight me on this."

"Can we table this conversation until after breakfast? I'm getting kind of hangry."

He chuckles, dropping my face and stepping back.

"Can you please go up and wake Libi? I'm surprised she's not already down here."

I cringe. "Maybe she's too scared to come out of her room. She probably heard us last night."

His brows shoot up as he considers it. "Maybe. It probably sounded like we were killing each other."

I snicker, and his eyes light up.

"Fuck. That's two days in a row that I've heard you laugh. Gotta be a record."

"Shut up." I shove his shoulder, flipping him off as I leave the room, hearing the rumble of his laughter follow me out.

Hurrying upstairs, I tap on Libi's bedroom door before I crack it open.

"Good morning, Liberty," I sing-song, stepping into her dark room despite the summer sun rimming the thick drapes like it's trying to fight its way in. "Your grumpy dad has cooked us bacon for breakfast."

I flick on the light, my gaze tracking across the generous room to the oversized white framed bed, dressed in pink sheets with white frills.

Shit. I forgot how extravagant Libi's room is. I was stunned last night when I put her to bed. It's like something out of a fairytale.

As I cross the space to the bed, I frown, finding it empty.

"Libi?"

I lift the blankets, as if I'd find her hiding under them like it's a Mary Poppin's bed, and the lumpy form of a five-year-old will magically appear.

"Shit, kid. Where are you?"

I drop the blankets and bend to check under the bed, only to find a sock and a Lego piece under there.

Straightening, I frown, my hands on my hips as I study the space. There are not many places to hide, so I check the one place that makes sense.

The little shit is probably trying not to laugh at me searching for her.

"Oh, Libi," I sing, tugging the walk-in wardrobe door open and flicking on the light.

My eyes quickly scan the space and my smile drops.

Shit. Nothing. That's weird.

Moving back out into the hall, I call her name. "Libi!"

Nothing. Huh.

This is a big house. I guess there are heaps of places to hide. So with that thought, I start searching.

The guest room is empty. So too is Tillie's room and the bathroom, so I go up to Kit's floor and check his room, office, and living area.

Still, I can't find her.

She must be hiding downstairs.

"Where's Libs?"

I spin at Kit's voice behind me in his private living suite.

"I don't know. She wasn't in her bed. I figured she's playing hide and seek or something. I've been searching, but can't find her up here. Figured she must be downstairs."

He frowns. "What do you mean? She hates hide and seek. Says hiding scares her."

He storms out of the room, and I kinda feel dumb, like I should have known that or something.

Tillie probably would have, but shit, I haven't spent that much time with the kid to know that sort of thing.

"LIBI!" Kit booms through the house as he opens and closes every cupboard, and searches under every bed.

I want to tell him that I've searched all the places he's searching, but every minute that passes has him even more frantic.

"Libi, this isn't funny!" he yells, rushing down to the ground floor. "Please Libi. Call out to Daddy!"

I hurry down, feeling the cold spike of panic seeping into my bones, because with every passing second, it's becoming more and more apparent that Libi isn't here.

"Libi!" I call, wishing I could do more, and as Kit rushes from the living room, through the kitchen and out into the garage, I follow.

I figure he must be going to check if she's in the car or something, but he hurries into another room off the side of the garage, and when I step in the doorway, I spot a wall of security monitors.

The heavy taps of Kit's fingers on the keyboard are loud and angry, and a moment later, the screens flicker to show the timestamp from last night, and me giving Libi a kiss on her forehead after I finished reading the book, and she'd dozed off in her bed.

The monitor follows my movements, tracking me through the house and back into the kitchen, while the top monitor in the corner shows Libi still asleep in her bed.

Kit fast forwards the feed, showing a very quick interaction between us in the kitchen, then me going upstairs to the first floor, where I start snooping through the house, and Kit finishes up in the kitchen.

Still, as he catches me in his room, the top monitor shows Libi still in her bed.

I stiffen as I realise there's actually a few cameras in his room, which means everything we did last night was recorded.

I don't know how to feel about that since he didn't ask permission. I would have said yes, but that doesn't matter right now. The only thing that does is finding Libi.

Kit runs the footage at high speed through about an hour of us fucking before he hits pause, a low growl rumbling from him.

Frowning, I peer closer at the screens, and it takes me a second to find what's got his attention.

In the far lower left corner, the monitor shows the backyard, and there on the screen are two black-clad figures, too big to be women.

You can't see their faces, their heads covered in ski masks, and as soon as Kit hits play again, we both watch them unlock the back door with a key, step in and disarm the security system, and walk right into the dining room by the kitchen.

Shit.

A shiver ripples up my spine at what this means, and I can hardly believe Kit is so fucking calm right now, because I'm about to start screaming in hysterics.

On the monitors, Kit follows the men as they move through the house, while Libi is still sound asleep in her bed, and well, at this point, Kit and I look like we are in a bloody MMA ring, grappling each other on his bed.

Oh. My. God. The men turn to look up the stairs to Kit's floor... like they can hear us.

"Kit..." I breathe. "Those men came in and took her, didn't they?" I can't hold back anymore, and Kit grunts in response, following them as they step into Libi's room and move to her bed, one man on each side.

My heart thrashes wildly in my chest as I step closer, my eyes zeroed in on the screen, to watch one man slap his hand over Libi's mouth, while the other injects something into her arm.

Cipher's hands are steady as he does his thing, slowing the security footage and making it less grainy as Wes and I watch over his shoulder.

I'm fucking livid. Red hot rage bubbles just under the surface, but I keep it locked down. Letting it go will only cloud my judgement. And when it comes to my Libi, I need to be crystal fucking clear.

"There." Cipher pauses the feed and zooms in on the screen. "See that fucker's sleeve? The one injecting Liberty? Look at his wrist."

I lean in close, as Wes whistles under his breath. "That's a dirty fucking move. Even for street trash."

Nodding, Julian, aka Cipher, glances over his shoulder at me. "Serpent."

"Yeah, I fucking see it," I snap, my fists balling, ready to fucking punch something. Anything. "I suspected as much."

The tattoo showing on the guy's wrist is still a little blurry, but it's clear enough to see the Serpents' signature tattoo of a snake head and a dragon head entwined together.

"The fuck do the Serpents want with a kid, mate?" Wes

barks, following me out of the security room as I storm back through the garage and into my house.

"The Serpents don't have an interest in Libs," I sneer. "Carlos does. He's been licking their boots, trying to climb the fucking ranks."

"Wait... Carlos, as in Rhonda's drug bag cousin?" Wes asks, and I nod as we step into the kitchen, my eyes automatically finding Bell, who is sitting at the kitchen bench, watching Colt lay out six laptops on the dining table.

"Yep. Rhonda got carted out of here by the cops last night," I explain, moving to the table to open my laptop. "My guess is her one call was to her gangster cousin."

As I boot up the device, a quiet lull washes over the room, and I glance up to see my team staring at Bell.

"What?" she snaps, and I'd smirk if I wasn't so fucking worried about my little girl.

"Who are you and why are you here?" Kade snaps, always the fucking prick.

I'm about to open my mouth to tell him to fucking check himself, but Bell beats me to it.

"I'm none of your fucking business. That's who I am."

This time, I can't fucking hide my smirk.

"Guys, this is Bell. Tillie's best friend," I explain, and Colt walks by her, giving her a nod. The kind of nod that could mean hi, or I'll kill you later.

That's about as social as Colt gets, so I'm impressed he gave her that much.

"Shit. Weren't you like a goth girl or something?" Wes smirks with his signature shit-eating-grin that has most people wanting to smack it right off his face, as he leans against the counter and he looks Bell up and down. "All black eyeliner and misery?"

Thank fuck the corners of Bell's lips kick up, taking no offense.

"I see my reputation precedes me." Her dark eyes flick to me. "You been telling your buddies about me, Kitty?"

I stiffen at the nickname as the guys fucking chuckle.

"Yeah-nah. He's kept you all to himself." Wes winks. "But I remember you from his wedding. When our fearless leader made the biggest mistake of his life and married the chick he knocked up."

"Hey!" I snarl, shooting Wes a fucking glare. "It was worth it for Libi."

"Yeah, yeah." He waves me off with a lazy flick of his wrist, his attention fixed on Bell. "Still... you were what? Sixteen? Seventeen?"

I can't help but sneak a glance at Bell to see if our age difference is going to be a fucking issue. There's nearly a decade between us. Nothing too fucking far-fetched, but still noticeable.

"Were you checking me out back then?" Bell crosses her arms over her chest and raises a dark brow at Wes. "Because I was sixteen at that wedding. Past the age of consent, but still, dude... that's creepy."

Wes's mouth drops open, and he can't string a fucking sentence together.

"What? I... shit."

Kade, aka Bruiser, bursts out laughing. "Oh, mate. She's got you good."

"Remind me to put 'verbal injuries' on your file." Garrick, otherwise known as Doc, snorts.

"Tragic." Julian smirks from behind his laptop. "The great Wildcard taken down by a teenage memory."

My eyes flick to Colt, wondering if the Ghost of our team has something to add, but all he offers is a slight twitch of his lips.

"Bell, we have some work to do," I mutter, shooting the guys a pointed look before they stop staring and move over to the table. "You're welcome to use my suite if you want to watch some TV."

Bell scoffs. "Unlikely. I want to find Libi too, you know."

"I know, but this stuff is... well..." I glance around my team, huffing out a breath. "Not exactly legal."

Her eyes widen with fucking excitement as a smirk pulls at one corner of her lips.

"Colour me intrigued." She gestures her head towards my open laptop. "Besides, you may need my expertise."

Chairs scrape as the guys sit, but I can't take my eyes off Bell's dark orbs, and the way they glisten with anticipation.

"What expertise is that exactly?" I ask, leaving the table to close the distance between us.

"I was voted Most Likely to Become a Serial Killer, remember? You might need me."

This time, my laugh is real but short, the dread in my gut overthrowing everything else, and Bell frowns, like she's perplexed.

"Why aren't you freaking out right now? Someone took Libi. Came right in and took her while we were—" She manages to stop before she says the word *fucking*, her eyes darting over my shoulder to my team. "While we were sleeping."

"Freaking out won't get my daughter back." My voice is flat, and I can tell by her softening eyes that she notices. "I know who took her. I just have to figure out how to get her back."

"But what if they hurt her?" Bell's voice cracks just enough to make the question worse, because shit, I can't think about that.

"They probably used a sedative." Garrick's steady voice cuts in from behind me as he approaches, holding his hand out. "Garrick Shaw. At your service, ma'am. But you can call me Doc."

For a long beat, Bell stares at Doc's outstretched hand like she's weighing up if she should shake it or chop it off before she finally accepts it.

"Bell Bishop. And if you call me ma'am again, I'll cut your dick off."

The room erupts in laughter as Garrick nods in defeat, not the least bit scared of Bell.

"Noted, Miss Bishop." He bows his head, his old-style tone not matching his rough appearance.

I almost laugh at how easily she gets under everyone's skin.

Almost.

"Right, if you're going to stay…" I trail off, gesturing to Garrick. "Garrick is our medic. He can stitch a man up with his eyes closed and make him swear it felt like a massage."

Doc shoots Bell a wink, and I point to the others, introducing them.

"You've kind of met Wes Wildcard Harlan." I gesture to my best mate as he pushes off the counter, his sandy hair mussed and bearded grin wide.

"Best fucking sharpshooter around, darlin'." He tips an invisible fucking hat towards her. "Nice to meet you."

Bell simply nods, glancing the way I gesture next.

"The grumpy prick is Bruiser. Youngest of us with skills of a fucking pro."

"I'm Kade Mercer," he grumbles, clearly not happy about Bell being here. "Call me whatever. I don't give a shit."

"Okay, shit-lips. And what do you do in this little gang?" Bell waves her hand around, and Bruiser fucking growls.

"Not a fucking gang. And I break shit and blow shit up."

Bell's brows hitch as she nods, impressed. "Nice."

"That's Colt Maddox. We call him Ghost on account of his stealth-like skills."

Colt doesn't bother with theatrics. He slips his hands into his pockets and gives Bell a single nod.

"Man of many words," Bell assesses, and fuck, she's spot on. "And you?" She glances at Cipher. "Let me guess. IT expert?"

"Julian Cross." He pronounces his name with every bit of upper-class Sydney that he was raised in, and I can tell by the way Bell's eyes roam over his clean-cut appearance that she's picking up the snob in him. "Tech is my specialty. I fight my wars online."

"You a hacker?" she asks, and he nods.

"One of the best."

"Huh. You might come in handy," she says vaguely, before glancing back at me. "So these are your old special forces buddies?"

"We met in the special forces," I nod, "but we still work together."

"Oh, yeah. In your security business." She air quotes the word security, rolling her eyes.

"Fine, since things have changed," I gesture between us, and she stiffens at the implication. "The Red Belly Team are mercenaries for hire."

"Well, stop fucking around and let's find Libi." She throws up her hands. "We have a black Christmas tree to buy."

I can't help but smirk at Bell, and as I close the two-foot gap between us and fist her dark hair, those dark chocolate eyes go wide in surprise.

"I meant what I said earlier, Bellicent," I mutter quietly so only she can hear. "When we get Libi back, we will be continuing this morning's conversation."

She doesn't say anything, simply staring at me as I release her hair and turn around to find Wes right behind me.

"Kit has been a bad boy."

"Fuck off, Wes," I mutter, shoving my best mate out of the way, and moving to the table.

We spend the next twenty minutes discussing strategy. Since we have no location of Carlos, we know we'll have to muscle information out of some of the lower gang members.

The only problem with that is how long it will take.

There's no evidence that they will hurt Libi. In fact, probably, once Rhonda gets out of lockup later today, I assume she'll use Libi as leverage to extort more fucking money out of me. After all, it's not the first time she's taken Libi. It's *only* the first time she got someone else to do it.

Doc assures me that if it was a sedative that was used, that Libi will probably still be sleeping, and not know what's happened.

He's only trying to make me feel better, but I know the guy well enough to know he doesn't even fucking believe his own words.

My little girl is only five years old, and some fuckers entered my house, with a fucking key, turned off the alarm like they had the pin memorised, and took her while I was busy living out my fucking sexual fantasies with Bell.

Doesn't matter the way you spin it. The real fucking crime here is how I've just failed fucking big time as a dad.

My phone pings with an incoming message, and I tug it out and open the message from an unknown number.

> She's a pretty little girl. All those dark curls,
> and those big fucking doe eyes. I took her as
> a favour to Carlos, but that fucker pissed me
> off, so now, she's all mine.

My fucking heart falls to the pit of my stomach as a photo comes through, and there, tied to a chair, wide awake with tears in her eyes is my beautiful baby girl, and on the floor by her feet, is Rhonda's cousin, Carlos, with his brain matter sprayed in chunks across the tiles.

A roar lurches from Kit as he throws his phone across the room, and I don't even get a chance to hear it hit anything or clatter to the ground before he has his laptop in hand, throwing it too.

Scurrying from my chair, a flashback slams into me of my father throwing his dinner plate across the room, sending food everywhere when he didn't like the taste of what my mother and I had prepared for him.

Air gets trapped in my lungs as he charges for me, and I brace myself knowing how badly his fists hurt, but the blow never lands. Not on me, because my mum leaps in front of me, taking each hit so I don't have to.

"Grab him!"

The bellow of a male voice shatters my memory, bringing me back to the present, and I find myself flush up against the wall, just like when I was little.

"Stop, Kit!" Wes yells, trying to leap on Kit's back, but the next thing to go is the dining table, the whole thing flipping to its side as he completely trashes the place.

My hands wrap around my throat as more air gets trapped in my lungs, and I know I'm not back there in that house with my parents, but I can't seem to shake the familiar feeling of terror.

The Red Belly Team works together to try to stop Kit from hurting himself, or anyone else, but I can't focus on him or the room we are in. Not when flashes of that shitty little kitchen with doors hanging off the hinges and the constant smell of stale cigarette smoke keep flashing before me.

Fuck, Bell. Calm down. Don't let him win.

All the self-talk in the world can't stop this from happening though. It's been years since I've been hurtled into a flashback panic attack, and I already know I'm too far gone.

Tears blur my vision making it hard to see, and my hearing is a combination of my pulse, and the numerous men yelling, but I manage to stagger to the door, feeling my stomach roll as I dart towards the powder room in the hall.

A loud gagging sob lurches from me as my hand wraps around the handle, and I only just manage to get the fucking thing open before the first waterfall spews from me, right into the toilet.

I'm sobbing as I purge, choking, not able to breathe, and I'm so sure that this time, I really am going to die.

It's different during sex. I get the high that comes with it. The pain and pleasure blend, but there's nothing about this that feels good.

It's pure torture.

A warm hand comes to my back, rubbing it, before a deep gravelly voice murmurs next to my ear.

"You're alright. You're safe."

I don't recognise the voice, but his touch, and his words, somehow help the panic to recede, and I stop choking on my own damn vomit.

"That's it," he says with the same rough but certain tone. "Focus on my voice. There's nothing here that will hurt you."

I do focus on his voice, his words having enough weight to

start to calm me. Even my purging eases as the room stops spinning and my body becomes my own again.

My hearing returns slowly as I expel one last time, my fingers white knuckling the toilet seat, and I pant, taking a moment to rest my head on my arm as I fully slump to the tiled floor.

There's no more shouting, but a little yelling, which is when I hear Kit's voice.

"Snake has her! He killed Carlos and said he's fucking keeping my little girl!"

Curses ring out, and I realise they are all coming from the hallway. Right outside the door. The fucking open door.

A handful of toilet paper appears in my vision, and I take it, wiping my mouth, before tossing it in and reaching up to flush all that vileness away.

"Jesus fucking Christ," Wes snaps. "Snake? As in the leader of the Serpents?"

"Who the hell else?" Kit roars, the fury in his voice echoing up the hallway. "You know any other cunts that go by that name?!"

I hear Kade growl something under his breath before Doc's voice cuts in with a sharp yell.

"Everyone shut the fuck up! Arguing won't help the kid!"

"Doc is right," Cipher's clipped tone follows. "I'll see if I can trace Snake's last known location. Give me some time."

As heavy feet stomp on the floor in the other direction, I shift back against the wall, my gaze falling on the big guy they call Ghost. Colt, I think his real name is.

He's on the floor too, knees up with his forearms resting on them, his hands dangling lazily as he watches out the door at his team.

Of all the people to come and comfort me, the quiet guy that looked like he wanted to behead me wasn't the one I thought it would be.

A set of feet move into the doorway, and my eyes travel up past the dirty shit kickers, and jeans with streaks of grease on them, to find a set of hands holding a glass of water, so soft looking I momentarily think they must belong to someone else.

Then my eyes meet the green stare of the one they call Doc. Their medic.

Well, now the soft hands make sense.

"Here, try to drink this."

He holds out the glass for me, and I take it, reading the concern in his gaze. He's studying me, something I don't particularly like, and when my eyes flick to Ghost, he nods towards the glass. So, I drink it. All of it.

"Do you have panic attacks often?" Doc asks, lowering to his haunches, and Ghost has to flatten his back against the wall where he sits next to me to allow Doc better access in the small space.

"I used to. As a teen. Haven't had one in a while," I mutter, my voice scratchy from purging.

"Yeah, I guess Kit's outburst triggered it," he says like it's no big deal, his big hands cupping my face as he tips my head back to assess my eyes. "You'll be okay, but I can give you some Xanax to take the edge off."

Shit. Xanax. I'm so tempted to say yes. To just let him give me something that will settle this fear still lurking in the back of my mind.

But no, I'm stronger than that. I have to be. I can't just throw away nine hundred and twenty days of sobriety because of one stupid panic attack.

So, I shake my head. "Thanks anyway, but I'm sober. I have to... feel everything."

Doc's brows shoot up as he gently releases my face, nodding before his eyes drift out the door, and I realise Kit is talking to him.

"Is she alright?"

"She'll be fine," Doc says, shifting to stand. "She's a tough one."

"Fuck… I know."

Something about the concern lacing Kit's voice has me relaxing, like a part of me thought he'd switched into a monster and would never switch back.

My dad never switched back. He was a monster with every breath he took.

Ghost stands, offering me a hand, and I take it, letting him pull me up on shaky legs.

"Trauma has a way of sneaking up on us," Ghost mutters past his dark facial hair. "We think we have a handle on it, and then it tests us."

"You're speaking from experience?" I ask, and he shrugs, but nods as his eyes shift out into the hall.

"Everyone here carries trauma. Some just hide it better than others." And with that, Ghost steps out of the room.

As I follow, I feel multiple sets of eyes on me, and all of a sudden it feels like the ink has melted off my skin, and all of my scars are visible. I haven't felt this vulnerable in years, and it has tears burning the backs of my eyes, making me want to shrink back inside the powder room to hide away.

"Bellicent."

Kit's voice is laced with pain, and my eyes lift to meet his, rimmed red and filled with agony.

"I didn't mean to scare you."

Jesus… he shouldn't be worrying about me right now.

"What are you talking about? You didn't scare me," I scoff, rolling my shoulders back and holding my head high. "I just didn't like you having all the attention."

The guys snicker, and slowly, Kit's lips twitch in the ghost of a smile.

"Get the fuck over here." He points to the floor in front of him, and the brat in me wants to say no, or make me, but shit, this guy has made me weak, and I don't know what to do about it.

Well, other than slowly walk over to him like his good little bitch.

"What do you want, Santa?" I practically purr, mentally latching onto my inner brat to try and normalise this very not normal situation.

I peer up at him through my lashes as I stand before him, ignoring the snickers of his mates, instead focusing on the deep growl that rumbles in his chest.

And then he kisses me. Right there in front of everyone.

I normally like a bit of exhibitionism, but that usually involves me naked and a dick or two, but this... kissing... it feels so intimate.

There are some hoots and hollers as Kit's lips brush mine. It's not a sexy kiss with tongue, but it's a kiss with care, reminding me how insistent he was this morning about telling Tillie about us.

Us.

Bloody hell. There is no us. It was one night. An epic night. But after Christmas, I'll be flying back to Melbourne, and he'll keep doing his mercenary stuff while raising his daughter.

Shit. Libi.

Kit pulls back suddenly like he's just thought the same thing, and the next second he's barking orders to his men as they follow him back into the kitchen and trashed dining room.

Whiplash. That's what this feels like.

I hover around the fringes of their heated debates, cleaning up here and there, listening to them argue about what to do.

They don't have a location on Snake, but they know he

frequents the Cronulla clubs, and every scenario they come up with ends up being too risky, because Snake is always surrounded by his Serpent crew.

It's clear to me that there's only one thing to do, and it doesn't involve the Red Belly Team at all.

I need to find this gang leader myself.

They don't call me The Seduction Slayer for nothing.

12

BELL

The problem with it being this close to Christmas is that the streets of Greater Sydney are jam-packed with last-minute gift shoppers, who are also consuming the ride-shares.

It took me forty-five minutes to get a car, and I was worried it would rock up right when Kit and his men arrived back at the house.

They went on an intel mission or something. But their absence gave me time to doll myself up and get my head in the zone while I reached out to some of my contacts to help me better pinpoint Snake's location.

Dion Abraham has been the leader of the Serpents for over five years. He got to the top by shooting his predecessor in the back of the head because he didn't like the way things were being run.

That alone explains this guy's mentality, and the fact he has Libi, who must be so fucking terrified right now, means we are walking a fine line. He could snap and hurt or kill Libi at any time. That's why I have to do this. For Libi. For Kit and Tillie. And for Snake's next innocent victim.

I usually spend weeks doing recon on a target. Learning

their habits and routines. But there's no time for that now. I need to infiltrate this Serpent gang, get close to their leader, and get to Libi.

As my ride slows in traffic, I lift my tits in my dress, so my nipples are nearly falling out. I don't have a bra on. In my experience, the outline of an erect nipple is hard for a man to dismiss, and I need whatever men I come across on this mission to go all gah-gah and think with their dicks.

Honestly, I feel a little sorry for them. They won't even see me coming.

The waterfront comes into view, people walking the streets in groups, laughing with friends or work colleagues as pink paints the sky.

Just like Melbourne, there are a lot of Christmas parties happening, some people already staggering, wearing off-centre Christmas party hats and tinsel leis.

I get dropped off along the main stretch, going into the first bar I see. It's already bustling with all the pre-Christmas celebrations, so I move to the bar and order myself a mocktail, sipping on it as I assess the crowd for what sort of girl I need to be in here.

I can't just be myself. Bell Bishop typically scares people away. But I've learned how to act in these situations, taking on a role to get close to people.

There are a lot of bubbly princesses in here, comparing their Christmas nails as they dance by their tables, not yet drunk enough to veer out onto the dance floor.

The men in here are all predictable. They eye anything with a set of tits. Thankfully, the air-con in here is up high, and my nipples are on high beam, making my piercings even more noticeable.

Spotting some guys with a Serpent tattoo weaving up their arms, I lift my mocktail and slip off the stool, dancing as I walk past, doing a fake little stagger before falling into one of the thugs.

"Ooopsss. Ssorrry." I giggle like an idiot, and the three guys who were ogling a couple of blondes at the next table turn their attention to me.

"It's okay, babe. You can run into me anytime." The curly haired dude I ran into beams, and I giggle again like he's the funniest fucker in the world. Meanwhile, I want to gag at how untrue that is.

"Ohh, you're cute." I pout as I press myself against him, resting my hand on his chest.

"So are you," he coos. "You looking for a good time?"

Jesus. He sounds like a hooker.

"Always. Are you it?" I ask too eagerly, and he nods.

"Fuck yeah."

"Max, we don't have time, man. We gotta head over to the local. Snake wants everyone there tonight."

Dammit. The local. That means a pub, but not which one.

On the bright side, I stumbled across these guys so easily. I just gotta get them to take me with them. Let them lead me straight to their leader.

"Oh, I wanna see your snake." I beam up at the curly haired fucker, and he does a little thrust against me that nearly has me gagging again.

"You want my meat, babe?"

Ugh. Extreme gag!

"Yeah. And your friends. Do you like to share?" I flutter my lashes while eyeing all of them, and just like that, they are putty in my hands.

"Fuck, man. Bring her with us. She'll fit right in." The guy who looks like he spends all of his money on crack shoots me a wink while cupping his junk, and I have to fight the urge to throat punch him.

"One look at her and the guys will want to run a train on

her." The other guy points out, but he doesn't sound like he's protesting.

No, this fucker thinks it's a good idea.

I mean, I don't mind a train as long as there's pain and humiliation, but from men I fucking choose to treat me like that.

These guys, who barely seem legal, are not the kinds of guys I'd put my trust in.

"I'll spread my legs for a train if you three line up first."

That's it. That's all I need to say before they are snatching the drink from my hand and leading me out of the bar.

I'm not concerned about their intentions, because I already know them.

They have no idea who they are walking up the street with. No idea who they are taking into their local. And no idea how there's a very big chance they won't make it to tomorrow alive.

We walk a few blocks, and I endure a groped arse and tit, and even Curly slipping his hand down the front of my dress to play with my nipple piercing, something that the three of them get way too excited about.

When we finally reach the local, which is the Prince Hotel, there is a thick crowd, so once we get inside and past the bouncers, I easily lose the three douches when we step into the thick of the crowd.

I wander the pub, finding the best vantage point on a staircase to look out over the main room, spotting the thickened crowd of Serpents gathered.

That's most likely where their leader is.

My phone vibrates in my small bag, so I check the screen to see numerous messages from the sender named Pussy.

Maybe I should change it to Throat Fucker?

Hmmm. Maybe later.

I open the tread, only reading the last one.

My heart sinks.

I didn't consider that he might be concerned for my safety. Now I kinda feel like a dick, but as the crowd parts, and I recognise the man from the profile my contact sent me about Dion Abraham, aka Snake, my worry falls away.

I found him. I'm going to get Libi back.

Glancing back down at my phone, I quickly tap out a text to Kit.

I hit send, and before I've even slipped my phone back into my bag, Kit is calling me.

I ignore it and head back down the stairs to weave through the thick crowd.

The music in here isn't really my thing, but I guess that's because a bunch of gang members and their chicks are here, rapping away with the lyrics while I have no clue what the hell they are singing.

I quickly see it's not going to be that easy to get into the inner circle of the gang, so I situate myself right at the walkway where they all seem to be coming in and out of a VIP area, and I lift my arms over my head and start dancing.

I'm better at dancing with someone. Grinding against them, letting our bodies roll together. But since I'm on my own and my target is out of reach, I imagine Kit is here with me.

I don't think I've ever seen him dance before, but given how he moves his hips when he fucks, I bet he can grind really fucking well against me to the beat of a song.

The trick to doing what I do is patience. Luring someone

takes time, so I get lost in my imagination for quite a while, swaying my hips, rolling my body, and closing my eyes to drown out everyone around me.

Every now and then, a guy comes up and tries to dance with me, but then I realise they quickly move off, and notice that the two security guys at the mouth of the VIP section are telling them to move on.

I grin at one, and then the other, but they don't smile back, instead, stiffening and turning away.

That's when I notice someone watching me through the crowd.

Dion Abraham.

He's on a lounge, relaxing back into it like it's his throne, a woman on either side of him, but while everyone around him talks, his eyes are glued to me.

Come on, Snake. Take the bait.

I turn my back, lifting my arms and swaying my hips, hoping my dress has ridden up enough to flash my red lacy panties.

"There you are." Curly pops up in front of me, and I hold back my eye roll.

"Oh, hey. This place is lit!" I call over the music, and he bites his lip as his eyes fall to my nearly spilling over tits.

"You're a fucking hot dancer. You work on a pole or something?"

Why are guys so dumb sometimes?

"Or something," I coo, pouting my lips into an air kiss before turning and snapping in half at the waist, pushing my arse against his crotch.

The moment Curly's hands land on my hips, two sets of feet appear before me, and I snap back upright, taking in the bouncers.

"Miss. Come with us, please," one says, and on the inside,

I'm doing an overexcited happy dance, but on the outside, I frown and pout.

"Are you kicking me out?" I whine like a little bitch. "I didn't do anything wrong."

Ugh, I sound so pathetic right now.

"Nothing wrong, darlin'. Our boss would like to see you."

"For fuck's sake. He can have anyone. Can't he just let me have her?"

The bouncers glare over my shoulder at Curly, before gesturing to the opening path to the VIP section, and I leave Curly behind, my eyes trained on my target as I approach him, giving my hips extra sway to make sure I seal the deal.

13

———

KIT

The fuck is she thinking?! Why would she willingly put herself in danger like this?!

"Which fucking club?!" I roar across the room where Cipher looks like he wants to tear my throat out.

"You know how many fucking clubs there are in Sydney and surrounds? She's a needle in a fucking haystack, mate! You want me to pull a miracle out of my arse too?" Cipher's fists are balled tight like he's seconds away from making it physical.

"Okay ladies." Doc steps between us with his palms raised. "Take a fucking breath before someone starts bleeding on the floor."

"You grew up with the fucking hob-knobs of this city, Julian," I snarl at Cipher. "Where the fuck do the gangsters hang out?"

Cipher's lip curls, his uppity accent breaking through as he speaks. "What? Because Daddy had a yacht, I must've snorted lines with the mobsters at the marina? Get fucked, Kit!"

Before I can throw another word at him, Colt's hand lands

flat against my chest, his ghostly silver eyes locking with mine.

"She's different."

Two simple words. But they silence the room, because when Ghost speaks, we fucking listen.

"Different how?" I snap. "Crazy different? Because you don't need to fucking remind me." I drag a hand through my hair, pacing.

"Not crazy." Colt shakes his head. "Intentional."

I stare at him, trying to decode whatever the fuck that means.

"Mate..." Wes moves up beside me, his eyes trained on Colt. "You keep saying that kinda spooky shit and I'm gonna start thinking you're clairvoyant. Besides..." he trails off, nudging me with his elbow. "Insulting our leader's new girl is a bad move, man. She's already scary enough sober."

Nobody laughs at Wes's attempt at humour, Colt's gaze flicking back to meet mine.

"She's got deep trauma," Colt explains. "But also, she creates it in others. I saw it in her eyes."

The entire room is dead silent for a few long beats, all of us trying to decipher his meaning, knowing it's important. I just can't figure out what the fuck he means.

"Pretend we are first graders, Ghost," Wes urges. "Spell it out for us."

Colt sighs like we are slow moving idiots and cuts to the point.

"She's a killer. Either a contractor like us, or... someone who picks victims for herself, following a pattern or routine, and may even leave a calling card."

I blink.

Then blink again as Wes starts laughing.

"Mate, are you saying she's a serial killer?"

I roll my eyes. "Bell Bishop is no fucking serial killer. She just likes people to think that, so they give her a wide berth."

Colt just shrugs. "I'm telling you what I see."

"Ghost seldom misses on this stuff," Bruiser points out from his lazing position in the armchair as he tosses a pinned grenade up and catches it again like it's a fucking tennis ball.

"So... what? You want me *not* to fucking worry about her?" I snap. "Snake, the fucking craziest leader the Serpents have ever had, not only has my little girl, but has my..."

"Has your what?" Wes wags his brows. "Yesterday morning you were single, mate. What the fuck happened last night?"

"Bell happened," I mutter, spinning away from my team to stare at the fucking shambles of the Christmas tree Rhonda trashed.

That bitch of a woman will pay for this.

For fuck's sake. Everything has turned to shit.

I've kept my distance from Sydney's gangland on purpose. I don't need that fucking shit in my life, and it's bad enough we often get hired by fucking mobsters, but gangs? Nah, those fuckers keep jobs in house, dealing with things themselves.

"You all have contacts. Reach out. Narrow the search. I want places the Serpents frequent." I turn back to my team, seeing them all nod, and fuck, even though I've been a total prick out of my mind with worry, they still have my back, getting their phones out and doing what I asked.

So, I fucking do the same.

My contacts are those mobsters I get hired by often. The last fucking thing I want is to owe them anything, but this is my kid, and my woman we are talking about. I'll do whatever it fucking takes to get them back safely.

Night has fallen over the city, the air still mild with the lead up to what's going to be a sweltering Christmas.

I feel like a fucking failure not knowing someone was in

my home stealing my kid right from under my nose. I'm supposed to have a fucking fortress, but in my desperation to drown in Bell last night, I didn't hear a fucking thing.

It's like those fuckers have the best luck, breaking in the one time I'm distracted—

Wait... Fuck... That can't be a coincidence.

Fuck.

"FUCK!"

"What is it?" Wes asks as I open my phone and hit Tillie's number, but I don't answer him, anger clouding my fucking vision as I wait for my sister to answer the fucking call.

"Have you found her?" Tillie's worried voice rushes out as soon as the line connects, still snowed in across the other side of the world.

"No," I snap. "But I need you to tell me more about Bell."

"Why? What's going on?" Tillie's voice turns high pitched, and my eyes flick to Wes as I speak.

"The one night I'm distracted by Bell, is the one night the Serpents come in and kidnap Libi. That's no fucking coincidence," I hiss, and Tillie is quiet for a moment before she speaks quietly.

"What are you saying?"

"I'm fucking saying, your psychotic friend did her best to keep me fucking distracted while those fuckers took my little girl!"

The roar of my voice booms through the living room, and each of my men glance at me, pausing their phone conversations as Wes curses next to me.

"Firstly, calling her psychotic is not an insult. She wears her trauma proudly," Tillie snaps through the line. "Secondly, why the fuck would Bell ever want to harm Libi? She doesn't even like kids, but Libi? She adores her."

I scoff at that, but Tillie isn't finished.

"And thirdly, how the hell did Bell distract you? Were you two arguing all night? Are you really that immature, Kitson?"

I ignore her questions, because fuck, that means admitting to fucking her best friend, and even though I want to talk to her about it, now isn't the fucking time. Especially when there's a high possibility I've been played, and Bell was in on it.

"Do you know what your best friend's favourite pastime is?" I snap, trying to steer the argument away from me falling for Bell's pierced nipples.

"Which one?" Tillie snaps. "The one where she works hard to stay sober, or the one where she lures men, seduces them, and slaughters them?"

I stiffen at her words, running them through my head over and over.

She didn't just say...

"She lures men?" I ask, remembering how she lured me, walking in here with that little black dress on that clung to her tits. How she came to collect on her *thank me later* tease, but fucking pretended like she wasn't interested. It's all part of her fucking game.

She lured me and seduced me, but she didn't slaughter me. Not in the physical sense, but fuck, my heart is shredded with Libi being taken.

"Jesus, Kit. Are you really that dumb? The Seduction Slayer. The serial killer that's been haunting Melbourne's men. All predators, I might add."

"The Seduction Slayer serial killer is Bell?"

"Shhhh!" Tillie hisses through the phone. "Not something you need to repeat out loud."

It's too fucking late. My team already heard it, but their eyes turn from me to Ghost, and a fucking chill ripples up my spine.

He fucking knew. That's what he was talking about before.

The fucker simply shrugs and returns to texting on his phone.

"Look, I'm just as worried about Libi as you are, but Bell has nothing to do with it." Tillie's voice draws my attention again.

"How the fuck do you know she didn't have anything to do with it?" I ask, turning away from my men to look out the front window and the glimmer of city lights in the distance. "You agreed she's a psycho."

"When you are someone she cares about, she would never harm you. She would kill for you, though. So the only thing you should be worried about is not if she helped orchestrate Libi's kidnapping, but what roles will she play in getting her back."

My heart sinks. Am I grasping at straws? Just trying to put the blame on someone else because I was the one who fucked up?

Maybe.

Wouldn't be the first fucking time.

Shit... I don't really think Bell had anything to do with this. She adores Libi. She'd never hurt her.

Bell Bishop isn't like other women, Kit!

"Bell's gone," I tell my sister. "Her last text message said, *'I'm as safe as a girl like me can be in a club full of gangsters.'* You know what that means, right?"

I hear my sister's sharp intake before she responds. "Yeah. Those gangsters are dead men. That's what that means."

"Be serious, Tills," I snarl. "If Bell is who you say she is, it means she's gone in without any intel on her mark, right? Like wouldn't she normally study her victim? Plan things?"

"Shit. Yeah. She does do that. She's very particular about

the setting. About the position and how it will look when it's discovered."

For a long beat, I'm fucking speechless.

"Kit? Are you there?"

I shake my head in disbelief. "You should analyse what you just told me and ask yourself if having a friend in your life like that is really alright."

Tillie scoffs. "She takes pride in her work. There's nothing wrong with that."

"You're missing the point," I snap as Cipher crosses the room to me and holds up his phone to show me a message.

> Serpents frequent Cronulla. Usually one of the pubs, but sometimes they go to the smaller bars and clubs. If you're looking for them, that's most likely where they will be. Cronulla.

"Fuck, gotta go, Tills. We just got a lead."

14

BELL

His eyes never leave me as I step into the VIP area and saunter towards the man they call Snake. As I get closer, his eyes drop down my body, taking in the sway of my hips, and the tattoo peeking from under my dress on my thigh.

Some guys don't like tattoos on women. Lucky for me, the Serpents' gang leader isn't one of them.

As I stop a few feet in front of him, popping my hip as I rest my hand on it, his lips part and he speaks to the women sitting on either side of him.

"Leave."

They both stiffen, their perfectly plucked brows shooting up as they throw him a questioning glare, but he pays them no attention as his bouncers step forward, each holding out a hand to the girls, and helping them to stand.

It's reluctant on their part, not hiding their pouts before one shoulder checks me on her way past.

Bitch doesn't realise I just did her a favour.

"I like the way you move," Snake drawls as he relaxes back on the sofa, stretching one arm out along the back.

And I'd like to see your head rolling across the floor.

"You do?" I ask like a ditz, trying to remain in character.

"Yeah. I do." He does that thing where he bites his lip like a fucking douche. "Haven't seen you round before."

I smile sweetly. "That's because I'm not from here. I'm visiting family for Christmas."

He nods at my lie. "Where are you from?"

"Melbourne," I answer easily, dropping my hand from my hip to start fidgeting with the strap on my bag, making myself look nervous when all I really want to do is tell him why I'm really here, and see his face as he realises death is coming for him.

"Melbourne, hey?" he asks. "What do Melbourne chicks like to do for fun?" He wags his brows in a disgusting way and I just want to stab him right now.

"Oh, you know…" I shrug. "Dance. Party." I emphasise that by running my hands up the front of my body, and his eyes flare as my fingers graze the sides of my tits.

"Dance for me," he demands, and just like he's expecting, I nod and start swaying to the music.

Lifting my hands above my head, I close my eyes as I roll my body seductively, and when I lazily pry them open, I find his eyes focused between my legs where my dress has lifted with the rise of my arms, revealing a hint of my panties.

"Come with me." He stands abruptly, and I keep dancing as I smile up at his towering height.

"Where are we going?"

"To party in private." His hungry gaze shifts away from me to his bouncers, not even caring if I say no as he starts leading me out of the VIP area.

Of course I don't protest. Getting him alone is exactly what I want. I'm a little disappointed it was so easy, if I'm being honest.

In a matter of seconds, he leads me through the club, past

the toilets, and out the back door that opens to the rear parking lot.

A car is already there, running, and he opens the back door for me, not gesturing for me to get in, but leading me to get in.

"Where are we going to party?" I ask sweetly, and a smirk kicks up his lips as he slides in beside me.

"My place."

"Which is where?" I ask, forcing a dash of worry in my tone to keep up with my sweet girl vibe.

"Don't worry, it's nice. A girl like you will love it. Probably never want to leave."

A chill runs up my spine at the implication that I'll never want to leave, because I realise, he means I'll never be leaving there.

He's definitely a predator. And given that he runs a gang, perhaps he's a trafficker too.

I do a fake giggle to cover up my shiver, and when he leans in like a creeper, trapping me against the seat to kiss me, I gasp in fake surprise, turning my head so his lips don't actually make contact with mine, the thought of him kissing me repulsive.

I instantly think of Kit, and how we kissed. It was anything but repulsive. I actually liked it, and a flutter of longing washes over me.

Kit.

I miss him. I miss being near him. I miss having his eyes on me. I miss hearing him call me Belladonna for Christ's sake. And I really miss riling him up.

Snake doesn't take my turn of head as rejection, his lips trailing down my neck as he palms my breast and gives it a painful squeeze.

I like pain. I usually get so turned on by it, which makes

times like this more tolerable, but right now, the pain brings me zero pleasure, and for a moment, I stop breathing.

Normally the pain is how I get through these events, forcing myself to get turned on... but shit. I'm as dry as a desert between my legs.

Am I broken?

Kit.

The moment Snake shifts back, fumbling for his fly while shoving my head towards his lap, I stop questioning these weird feelings I'm having and focus on the task at hand.

Right now, that's a blowie.

This is what I do. I seduce. Let them think I care or am attracted to them. Give them the attention they crave so they let down their guard. And then, I strike.

I don't particularly like this part, but I have to use what I have, and that's a set of tits and a plump set of lips that most men can't help but imagine fucking.

I endure his foul semi hard foreskinned dick surging between my lips as I start sucking him off, and for the first time ever, I feel like... I'm cheating.

Wait, what?

Cheating? That would imply I have a boyfriend or something. Which I don't.

Kit's blue eyes flash through my mind. The intensity in them as he told me he was going to tell Tillie that we are a thing... or something.

I'm so confused. Did I agree to that?

I don't think I did, but all I wish right now is to be back in that room arguing with him about it. Perhaps letting things get a little heated, and we'd end up without any clothes.

I can't help but think of Kit's bendy dick and how it made me gag so damn good last night.

This dick currently in my mouth is gross, and not

completely hard and just... well, now I'm fighting a gag, and not because he has a bendy dick that hits my reflexes.

Since I know gagging turns guys on more, I fake a gag, and just like I knew it would, it spurs him on, making him thrust faster. It's not only fast but also brutal, and I can tell he's trying to hurt me as his fingers fist into the back of my hair as he holds my head in place.

"Fuck yes. You slut. Gag on my huge cock."

I do gag, and it's not fake, and it's not because he hits the spot, or because his dick is huge... that fucking thing is smaller than a brush handle.

I gag because he really is that repulsive.

I can hardly believe my reaction, and I consider that Kit has finally broken me completely. I'd much rather be thinking about him, but this vile prick fucking my mouth starts to hammer into my throat, and I know what's coming.

Another gag, this one fake, and he goes rigid as hot jets of cum shoot into my mouth.

I cringe at the acidic taste, gagging for real again, and I refuse to swallow a single drop of this rancid seed, so I let it coat his dick, trying to keep more on him than in my mouth.

It's then that I notice the car slowing to a stop, and the moment he releases my hair, I jerk up with a gasp, seeing we are parked in a dingy double garage.

Well played, Mr Abraham. You distracted me on purpose. Now I have no fucking clue where I am.

"Where are we?" I pant, my voice hoarse from having my throat brutally fucked moments ago.

"My place. Just like I told you before," he grumbles this time, the charming persona he spoke with when we were chatting in the VIP area of the Prince Hotel now long gone.

I giggle like a clueless idiot. "Oh, I know that, silly." I slap his thigh playfully. "I mean, where is your place? What suburb are we in?"

"We are still in Greater Sydney, love," he says, tucking his now flaccid dick back into his pants. "That's all you need to fucking know."

I want to stab the creeper now. It takes everything in me not to. But I know I can't. Not yet. I need him alone and to find out where Libi is. And only then can I make him pay.

Clutching my purse at my side, I let him roughly drag me from the car like I'm his prisoner, not his guest, and the two bouncer dudes appear by the entrance door, like they magically teleported from the pub.

I'm hoping my poker face is well in place right now, because on the inside, I'm definitely frowning.

How the hell did they beat us here?

They weren't in the car with us. They must have been ahead of us, but then again, they were standing in the parking lot when we pulled away.

This is not my first rodeo, so it's entirely possible that while Snake kept me busy with my head in his lap, unable to see the passing streets out the window, the fifteen-minute drive could well have been a series of blockies to kill time and throw me off.

It's the only way to explain why the bouncers are here before us, which means we are still in Cronulla. Or close to it.

That also means I'm still a long way from Kit.

Snake leads me into a house that was absolutely built in the eighties and hasn't seen a lick of redecoration since. The bouncers follow as I'm led with a strong grip around my upper arm, down a long hallway, passing a kitchen where a group of thugs bag up coke, before leading me into a long narrow living room.

My eyes instantly find the lines of white powder on the table, like they were left behind like leftovers from dinner.

Instantly my mouth goes dry, and I drag my gaze from the coke as my heart begins to race.

Just don't think about the coke, Bell. Think about the kill. How good that rush will be.

"Drink?" Snake asks, moving to a small rickety drinks trolley.

"No thanks. I'm good." I smile sweetly when he glares over his shoulder at me.

"I thought we came here to party," he hisses, and I lazily smile while waving him off, moving to the bay of windows to peer out into the night.

Where the hell am I?

"I've already had so much to drink," I lie. "Any more and I'll be a lazy lay."

He doesn't even laugh.

Fucking hell. Tough crowd.

"One more won't hurt," he remarks, and the finality in his tone has me stiffening.

Shit. This guy is either paranoid, knows why I'm really here, or is a worse predator than I thought.

Refocusing my eyes, I stop looking out the window and look at the reflection on the glass, watching him pour two glasses of scotch or whiskey, and then proceed to break apart a capsule into one of them.

Shit.

Not only can't I drink the alcohol, but he just spiked it with something that I absolutely can't have. I'm sober, for fuck's sake. I can't drink that. I can't!

My heart thrashes wildly in my chest as panic for the second time today grips me.

It's been years since I've felt this out of control. One night in Kitson Hall's bed and I'm a fucking mess. I should be able to handle this situation. Instead, it's freaking me the hell out.

Where the hell is the killer in me when I really need her?

It's the drugs. It's thrown me off, and I'm not too proud to admit that maybe I'm a little out of my depth here.

I've done zero research for this mark. I have no idea what this guy is really like, but I know by the way he watches me as I turn back to face him, that every thought running through his head is sinister.

"You like kids?" he asks out of the blue, and I glance around again looking for any sign that he's a dad, and kids reside here. All I find is his two bouncers standing in front of the door, which is the only way out of this room. The other door leads into a small powder room, the light already on and more lines of coke dusting the bench by the sink.

I shrug as I find nothing hinting to kids, glancing back at him. "They're okay, I guess. Not really my thing."

He nods once and holds out a glass that I know is spiked, and I shake my head.

"Oh, you didn't hear me?" I play dumb. "I don't want a drink, thanks."

"And you mustn't have heard me. I said, one more won't hurt," he sneers, stepping closer with the glass still held out to me. "Have a drink with me. Relax."

His insistence is a huge red flag, and I know if I drink that I'll be more than relaxed. I'll be out of it.

Nine hundred and twenty days.

Nine hundred and twenty days.

Nine hundred and twenty days.

"I'm plenty relaxed." I wave him off with a pathetic giggle. "Are we going to fuck here or your bedroom?"

Come on, Snake. Take the bait. Get that horrid cock out again and start thinking with it.

"We will fuck right here," he smirks, raising the glass a little higher, "after you drink this."

I giggle stupidly again. "You're so bossy. Are you like a Daddy Dom or something?"

Ugh, if I have to play this dumb bitch for much longer, I'm going to cut out my own tongue.

"Or something." Snake's smile is toothy, and for the first time I notice that some of his teeth are decaying badly.

A nauseous hot sweat blooms at the back of my neck at the thought of having to go near him again.

But I have to. I have to find Libi.

"Here. Have the drink and we can get started." Snake approaches, moving to hand the glass to me, but I quickly move away, walking towards the bathroom.

"I need to pee first."

If I can get in there, I can call Kit. Send him my map location and get the fuck out of here.

The words, "stop her," meet my ears, but I don't look back as I rush for the small room, and right as I'm about to step inside, two sets of brutal hands grab my arms and haul me backwards.

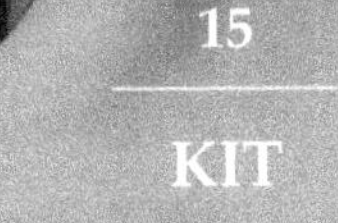

15

KIT

It only takes us twenty minutes bar hopping in Cronulla to find the bulk of the Serpent gang partying at the Prince Hotel. They are fucking everywhere. But you know who's not fucking here?

Snake. Or Bell. Or Libi.

Fuck.

FUCK!

"You know, Bruiser could have this place rigged up in under half an hour," Wes says next to me, pretending to sip on a beer. "I could position myself across the street on the rooftop to take out any stragglers that manage to escape the explosion."

"As soon as I find Libi and Bell, then fucking go for it," I mutter, feeling my palms sweat with the urge to kill every motherfucker in here.

"Cipher to Viper." Julian's voice crackles in my earpiece.

"Go ahead," I mutter, knowing he can hear me.

"I'm locked into the security system here. Nothing untoward is happening right now, but I've gone back through the footage for the last hour and can confirm that your slayer was here and left with Snake about thirty minutes ago."

"Fuck, Bell. What are you doing?" I mutter to myself, knowing my whole team can hear me on comms, but not fucking caring.

"Can you track the car?" Wes asks for me since my head isn't real fucking clear right now.

"I tried but lost it," Julian mutters. "I'm currently back-tracking to follow his security. They left at the same time, but on foot. I'll let you know as soon as I find anything."

"Copy that," Wes mutters before Cipher goes offline.

"Ghost to Viper." Colt's deep but gentle voice comes through the comms next. "I have eyes on Snake's right-hand Serpent. You wanna have a chat with him?"

I smirk, meeting Wes's eyes as I nod and respond. "Fuck yeah. Snatch the fucker and let's show him how the Red Belly Team likes to party."

"Copy that," Ghost says, and suddenly, the panic inside me starts to recede.

Mattier Arnold, aka the Mad Hatter, is not only Snake's right-hand man, but his best buddy. If Snake has either or both of my girls, this fucker will know about it.

Wes and I brush off about six fucking attempts by hammered chicks on our way through the pub and out the rear doors to our waiting van.

Inside, we find the rest of my team, as well as a bound and gagged Mad Hatter, and the moment I close the door, Doc is speeding us away from the Prince Hotel to find a nice, secluded place for our little party.

The drive takes about twenty minutes and gets a little bumpy as we near Potter Point, but it's the perfect location where the roar of the waves crashing against the rocky cliffs will drown out any screams. There are no houses or buildings out here. Just sandy walking tracks and rocky cliffs that roll down into the ocean.

I'm in no mood for fucking around, so we have Mattier

out of the van and on his knees on the ledge of the rocky cliffs in a matter of minutes, Doc and Ghost blinding him with torches so he can't see us properly, as I fit the silencer onto my gun.

"Where's the girl Carlos brought to Snake?" I sneer, and right as Wes rips the tape off Mattier's lips, he spits in my direction.

"Fuck you! I will never tell you where she is!"

I pull the trigger, his cry more of a gasped gurgle as the bullet tears through his shoulder.

"I'll ask again. Where's the girl?"

"Fuck you." He grunts in pain. "Snake will gut you for this."

I scoff. "I will gut you if you don't tell me what I need to know."

"All you need to know is your little girl might not be so innocent before the night is through."

I want to blow his fucking head off, but I need intel, so I fight that fucking urge and blast through his thigh this time.

His cry is higher pitched this time. Probably because I shot him so close to his fucking nuts.

Every time I ask him a question and he refuses to answer, I shoot something of his. His wrist, his fingers, his gut, making sure it's just a flesh wound so he won't bleed out straight away.

The moment I press the silencer barrel to his dick, he speaks up.

"H-he went h-home with a chick," Mattier sobs. "H-he lives four blocks from the Prince Hotel. Tobias Street. Number s-seven."

"The chick he was with. She have dark hair and a chest tatt?" I snarl, and he nods quickly.

"Y-yeah. Her ink travelled up her throat. Had more tatts on her arms and legs."

That's my Bell.

"And the kid, is she there too?"

He shrugs. "I dunno. He doesn't fill me in on his pedo stuff."

My fucking veins turn to ice. Why the fuck would Rhonda do this to her daughter? Why would she get her cousin involved? It was always gonna turn fucking bad. What the fuck was she thinking? Why did she think it's okay to expose her daughter to this shit?

Fucking hell. I already know the answer.

Money.

That cunt of a woman is going to die for this.

"Stand him up," I demand, and Wes and Ghost do as I ask, helping the bleeding fucker stand with only one leg uninjured.

"Just leave me here," he pleads. "By the time I get help, you'll be done, and I won't be able to alert them that you're coming."

I lift the gun and press the barrel to his forehead, right between his brows.

"Please. You don't have to shoot me," he sobs, and a twisted chuckle leaves my lips.

"I know."

I shove the gun forward, pushing him back, and in a few stumbling steps, he falls right over the edge of the cliff, down into the murky waters of the Pacific Ocean.

16

BELL

Thug one and thug two have me pinned to the back of the couch as Snake looms over me, his top lip curling like I'm the one that disgusts him.

"I told you to have the drink. It was a simple fucking request. Why do you have to make this so difficult?"

His spittle slaps against my cheek, and I fight the urge to snap at him like a rabid dog. I may be in a bit of a predicament right now, but I don't need him knowing that side of me just yet.

I might kill people for the love of it, but the only skills I've needed up until now were seduction and taking them by surprise.

I'm not trained to fight. I can scrap like any chick, but I'm no match for two hulking bouncers and a feral gang leader.

"What are you doing?" I cry out, hoping I sound scared, and well, in all honesty, I kinda am. "I need to pee so we can fuck. Isn't that why I'm here?"

"Drink first, then you can pee and I'll fuck you unconscious."

Shit. That's exactly what I like, but for the first time, I don't want it. Not with him. Not with anyone but

Shit.

Fucking hell, Kit. What have you done to me?

"I thought you were cool," I whimper, trying a different angle. "We are here to party. There's no need to manhandle me. I'll be your sex slave for the night."

Snake and the two bouncers chuckle like I just told a fucking joke, all of them looking down at me as the dude on my right side digs his fingers into my arm bruisingly as he holds me in place.

"I don't need you to be my sex slave," Snake sneers, leaning so close that his hot foul breath mingles with mine. "I have plenty of those. Now stop fucking around and drink this or I'll force it down your throat."

My heart begins to thunder in my chest at the thought of being drugged. I can't let him do that to me. I need to end this somehow.

Nine hundred and twenty days.

"Okay," I snap. "I'll drink your damn drink, but you'd better give me the best orgasm for treating me like this."

God, could I sound any more bimboish?

Snake's eyes narrow before he nods to his bouncer buddies, and they release their hold.

"You say you want to party, but you won't do coke with me or have a drink. Seems a little off to me," he snaps, and I shrug, fluttering my lashes as he holds the glass out again.

"I'm just pacing myself." I smile up at him even though I want to dick punch him.

Hey, now there's an idea.

I accept the glass from him, and he takes a step back, finally giving me space.

With his arms crossed over his chest, he stares down at me, waiting, and I quickly contemplate my next move.

Dumb and Dumber have backed off, but they are still

lingering behind me, too close for comfort. If I try to run, they'll be on me before I even lurch up off this shitty couch.

My eyes land on my purse laying forgotten on the floor just outside the powder room. My phone is in there, plus a knife, but I have two others concealed in my boots.

"I'm sick of fucking waiting. Drink the fucking drink!" Snake bellows, making me flinch.

I roll my eyes and lift the glass to my lips, the scent of whiskey teasing my taste buds.

Shit, what I'd give to feel that burn. To let the alcohol relax me.

Nine hundred and twenty days.

With my eyes trained on Snake, I tip the glass against my lips, knowing I have two options here.

The first is I drink it. Throw my sobriety out the window to protect myself, all while putting myself in more danger, because once the drugs kick in, I know I'll be useless.

The second is tossing the drink and trying to make a run for it, knowing they'll likely catch me and drug me, anyway.

The first option is the most obvious, but the problem with that is I'm a fighter, and no one dictates my sobriety other than me. So if I'm going down, then I'm going down swinging.

Without second guessing myself, I hurl the glass at Snake's head and leap off the couch, hearing it clunk against his head before smashing to the floor.

"Get her!"

The bouncers shout as they come for me. I make it five steps before someone slams into my back, sending us crashing to the floor.

The weight of one of the thugs crushes me, and I try to squirm, reaching for my purse that's only a few short inches away, but shit, those inches feel like miles.

"You fucking whore!" Snake yells, shoving the thug off

me before slamming his foot into my ribs. "I knew you were up to something! Are you a fucking cop?!"

I wheeze out a strangled whimper as my winded lungs fight for air, and Snake flips me over on my back as he and his bouncers loom over me.

"You didn't just start teasing me randomly. You fucking sought me out. Who are you and what do you want?!"

I part my lips to speak, but I'm still struggling for air, so I lift my hand and uncurl my middle finger, flipping him off.

He snarls before his foot comes down on my head, pain bursting through my skull as my vision wavers.

"Cunts like you deserve everything you fucking get," he hisses before glaring at his thug buddies. "Fucking hold her in place."

My head is dazed and fuzzy, feeling heavy as it lolls to the side to see my purse so close.

Kit... I'm sorry.

For some stupid reason, I think I have the power to send him that message telepathically, but I hope he knows I died trying. I died fighting for his little girl.

Hands and knees hold me down onto the grotty brown carpet, and I try to fight, but my limbs are just as heavy as my head.

Shit. Am I even still alive?

Snake appears over me, kneeling down with something in his hands.

"All the women beg. First it's, *no don't drug me*, and then it's *please give me more.* You're all the fucking same, only good for a warm hole to fuck and a mouth to abuse." He nods to one of the brutes, and the next thing I know, my lips are being pried open by fat calloused fingers before Snake holds up the bottle of whiskey and starts pouring it into my mouth.

Tears spring from my eyes as I fight to keep my throat

closed, but the second someone pinches my nose, I know it's useless.

Since I'm so good at breath play, I'm able to hold out longer than they must be used to, but Snake gets impatient, punching my gut, and I instantly start choking as the burn of the whiskey breaches my throat and goes down.

"No!" I cry as I hack, while the three of them fucking laugh. "Please stop! I'm sober."

I choke on another cough as the three men stop laughing.

"Really?" Snake asks in surprise. "Well, why didn't you just say so?"

If I thought he was going to be kind or understanding, then I'm dead fucking wrong, because with another nod, my arm stings with the prick of a needle, and I gasp, spotting the reddish contents disappear into my arm as Snake laughs.

"There we go," he pat-slaps my face. "No longer sober. Now you don't have to keep fighting it."

Fuck.

No, no, no.

Nine hundred and twenty days wasted.

NO!

I struggle and fight against them, but they keep me in place, and I'm well aware they are doing it on purpose to let the drugs and alcohol take effect.

It was reddish in colour, so not something I recognise.

They talk amongst each other for a minute even while the two thugs hold me down, and a heavy rush starts to wash over me, making me feel so fucking good, but not enough that I don't feel the weight of what's just happened.

I cried from fear and panic earlier today, but now, as my silent tears fall, I cry because I'm absolutely gutted.

I'd worked so hard to get clean and stay clean. I may have picked up other unhealthy habits in place of my substance addictions, but in my defence, the people I slaughtered were all bad people. Paedophiles. Rapists. Women killers.

Serial killing bad people is less selfish than spending every waking moment seeking out my next hit of drugs.

The rush finally hits hard, and the bouncers release me, leaving me on the floor.

My eyes drag to my purse nearby, but as I reach for it, rough hands pick me up as Snake issues an order.

"Lock her up with the other one and keep checking on her. Any sign that the sedative is wearing off, start shooting her up with a Spaceball. If she's an addict, she's gonna need more than the typical bitch we steal off the streets."

I try to open my eyes as the lightweight of bliss sends me soaring, and I don't even think I'll make it to where they intend to lock me up, as something close to heavenly death grips me, and everything goes black.

BELL

The feel of cool, gentle fingers brush over my forehead, and the weighted fog starts to lift as I try but fail to pry my eyes open. I feel so heavy.

"Bell?"

The small, scared voice at my ear has my sluggish brain trying to fire up, but the path to it is blocked.

"Bell, please wake up."

Shit. Am I hallucinating?

"Please," the voice whispers through a sob. "Wake up. I want to go home. I want my daddy."

I can't be hallucinating. She sounds so real.

Slowly, I manage to open one lid to see a blurry head of dark hair hovering at my side.

"Bell?"

"Libs," I mumble as relief washes over me. "You okay?"

A loud sob escapes her. "I want my daddy. Please," she cries, clawing at my arm like she never wants to let go. "I just want my daddy."

I never knew my heart could break while woozy like this, but it fucking does.

"Help me... sit up," I slur, forcing my other eye open, and

Libi stands tugging frantically on my arm. Her small five-year-old strength hardly helps at all, but the fact she's here, and alert is what fuels me to push off the cold concrete floor.

"What's wrong with you?" she asks, hiccupping on another sob.

"The bad man forced drugs into me, sweetie. I'll be alright," I mutter, leaning forward to reach for my boot, pulling out the first blade from the heel, and then the other.

The room spins a little, and another round of relief washes over me as I realise I was injected with a sedative, and not something more potent. It was probably a fast-acting sedative, and I wonder if that's what they used on Libi when they kidnapped her.

Probably.

"Is that a knife?" Libi asks, her little socked feet move into my line of sight, and I nod, glancing up to look at her.

She's still in her black nightie with a skull head reindeer on it.

Fucking hell. How could anyone want to hurt or scare this beautiful little angel?

Her dark curls are a wild mess, and her big blue eyes are brimming with tears, those rosy cheeks soaked like she's been crying for hours.

She must have been so scared.

"Your eyes look funny, Bell."

I drop them from hers as I nod, hating that I probably look a little drunk.

"It's the drugs, Libs. They are making it hard for me to move fast."

"I'll help you." She holds out her hand, and I smile, I think, moving the two blades to my left hand while placing my right in her outstretched palm.

I take in the space as Libi holds my hand. It's a small room that looks like it's meant for storage, but there's nothing in here but a couple of buckets, a stack of cardboard boxes, and a sink.

Shit. A sink.

Dropping Libi's hand, I rush over to it, testing the tap, and putting my blades down on the edge, smiling when it turns on. Bending, I drink straight out of the faucet, the cool rush of water an instant relief as it fills my mouth and I drink it down, hoping it will help to rehydrate my veins and flush the sedative faster.

Probably won't but fuck it, that's what I'm telling myself.

I finish up by splashing my face with the water, and then offer Libi some, hoisting her up a little so she can duck her head into the sink to drink the same way I did.

I don't know how long she's been here or if they've fed her, but I need her strong so we can try to escape.

When she's done, I lower Libi back to the ground, turning off the water to look over her. Lowering to my haunches, I run my hands over her head and arms, checking for wounds, but nothing seems amiss.

"Did they hurt you?" I ask her, my eyes locking with those big blue ones that are still swimming with fear.

She shakes her head and starts crying again. "No. I just want to go home."

"I know, sweetie." I cup her little face and brush over her wet cheeks with my thumbs. "You'll be back with your daddy in no time. I promise. Okay?"

She nods, completely trusting me, so I pull her into my arms and hug her close.

My eyes flick to the door to find three locks which makes escaping unnoticed out of the question.

Shit. This is a fucking conundrum if I ever saw it.

Now would probably be a good time to completely admit that I've fucked up. I did no research. No habit tracking or routine stalking. Just went in all bloody willy-nilly, and now,

I'm locked in a room in a house somewhere south of Sydney.

The sound of heavy feet coming our way has us both stiffening, and I lurch up, pushing Libi towards the far corner and snatching up my blades.

Libi starts crying again, slapping her own hand over her mouth as she pushes herself flush into the corner, her little eyes terrified as they remain locked on the door.

Fuck.

I hate this.

I hate seeing her so scared.

If these fuckers have done something to her—

The sound of locks clicking open has me moving, and I rush over to Libi, spinning to face the door just as it slams open, bouncing off the wall.

A screech flies from Libi behind me, and I manage to hide the knives behind my back as I try to make myself bigger to hide Libi.

"Time for a top up," one of the bouncers from earlier grunts, holding something up, and when he steps into the room, the moment the light hits him, I see the syringe.

Shit. I know what that is. It's not the reddish colour of whatever sedative they injected me with before. It's white.

Cocaine.

My heart flips at the sight of the drug of choice from my past.

Shit. Shit. Shit.

No. I don't want that. I don't.

"Stay back!" I yell, curling my lip as I bare my teeth, and I see the moment he realises I'm not the same damsel from the living room before.

"She has bark now." He laughs. "But does she bite?"

He steps further into the room, and Libi shrieks from behind me.

"Get away!"

Spinning quickly to face her, I take her hand and wrap her tiny palm around the hilt of one of the knives.

"If he comes near you," I whisper quickly, "stab him in the eye with this."

She sobs but nods as I spin back to see the thug heading my way, and I quickly shuffle along the wall to put space between me and Libi.

"You can't escape me," he chuckles, like this is a game of chase.

"That's funny," I sneer. "I was just thinking, *you* can't escape *me*."

His brows hitch momentarily as confusion settles over him, and I see the cogs in his brain working as he slowly thinks about what's happening here.

Whatever conclusion he comes to is the wrong one, because the idiot lunges for me.

The drugs in my system are still making me a little sluggish, so my reaction time is delayed, and I don't get to swing the knife before the needle digs into my neck. But then, as he begins to inject it, I swing my hand and stab, and stab and stab, feeling him jerk with each plunge of the knife.

The rush of hot blood pours over my hand as I keep going, feeling the needle fall from my neck and clatter to the floor.

"Bell!" Libi cries from the corner as the thug and I go crashing to the ground, but I don't stop stabbing, knowing her life depends on me.

I can't stop. I can't give up. I have to make sure he's dead. That he can't drug Libi too. I have to keep her safe.

A gurgling sound meets my ears, and I try to focus my blurred vision, taking in the bouncer lying on his back in a pool of blood.

My knife and my blood-soaked hands come into view

next, moving slowly before my eyes as I study how bright the blood is against my skin.

Shit.

I glance over at the syringe on the floor to see he managed to inject half of it.

Cocaine shouldn't make me sluggish like this though.

Snake's words from earlier filter in...

"Shoot her up with a Spaceball."

Fuck. A Spaceball... that means the coke is laced. Most likely with fentanyl.

"Bell!" Libi's desperate cry drags my sluggish attention to her, and she points over her shoulder as a loud crash and yelling come from outside the room. "They're coming!"

Fuck. I need to focus.

"Stay here," I rush out, feeling my heart start to race, and I quickly stumble to the open door.

"Don't leave me!" Libi cries, and my blood smeared hand grips the door as I turn back to look at her.

"I'm not leaving you, Libs. I'll be back. You stay here, and stab anyone that tries to get close to you."

I don't wait for her to respond, hearing feet rushing down some stairs, and I glance up the passage to see a man I don't recognise running my way.

There's a fair chance I'm going to die here tonight, but I'll go down slaying.

I smirk at that thought, the drugs obviously clouding how bloody dire this situation is.

But hey. I'm The Seduction Slayer. And tonight, I'm Slaying for Santa.

"How'd you get out?!" the idiot yells, rushing at me, obviously not seeing my blood coated hands on the knife in my death grip.

"Your buddy. You should fire him. He's bad at his job."

The guy frowns as he reaches me, and before he can comprehend what's happening, I slash the knife across his throat.

Blood sprays across my chest as his eyes widen, panic contorting his features as he stumbles back, his hands instantly pressing to his throat, but it's no use. My blades are sharp, and neck slashing has become my thing.

The adrenaline rush of what I just did spurs me on, and even though I know something like fentanyl is coursing through my veins with the half dose of coke, I still seem to be able to function enough to get the job done.

More rushing feet start coming down the stairs as someone yells to get the kid, so I duck into the closest open door, waiting for my next victim to appear.

"Hey, Azza! What the fuck are you doin—"

His words cut off as he passes the doorway I'm hiding in, his eyes trained on his gang mate bleeding out on the floor.

"What the fuck."

And that's my cue.

Stepping out, I reach up and tap the guy on the shoulder, readying myself as he spins in a panic to look at me.

Slash.

Shit. This really is too easy.

More blood coats me as the guy slides down the wall and he gargles, drowning in his own blood.

Well... this is fun—

A hard body slams into me from the side, and I go crashing to the floor as the sound of a war erupts on the floor above me.

"You fucking whore!" another unfamiliar voice snarls, fisting the back of my hair, and slamming my head to the floor.

Pain bursts through my skull, and darkness rims my vision, but the sound falling from my lips is a deranged laugh.

"You idiot," I laugh, and he lurches off me, giving me space to roll over and look up at him. "Don't you know how much I love pain. Keep roughing me up like this and I'm gonna come."

"The fuck!"

He lunges for me again, and I go to swing my knife, only now realising I don't have it anymore.

Whoops.

Spinning on the floor, I scurry on my hands and knees over my second victim, rushing for the open door of the room Libi is still huddled in.

"You like pain, do you?" the guy says before a boot comes down hard on my back.

I cry out as the pain hits, following it up with a laugh even as tears fill my eyes.

Okay. So maybe this isn't so fun.

I like pain... in the bedroom.

I especially love it coming from Kit's hands, or teeth, or dick... dammmmnnn. Kit.

Now flat on my stomach, I cough and wheeze, deciding antagonising this guy needs to wait until I have a knife in my hand, so I army crawl to the open doorway.

"I was told not to kill you, but you have to fucking pay for killing a Serpent."

I ignore him, dragging myself through the door, my eyes finding Libi, curled tightly in a ball in the corner as she rocks herself, her big eyes locking with mine.

"Knife." I reach out towards her, the four metres of space

between us feeling more like a football field. "Toss the knife to me."

Libi whimpers as another heavy kick lands in my ribs, and I scream as I feel them crack, bending in half as the clatter of the knife meets my ears, falling short.

Shit!

I have to get to the knife. If I don't kill this guy, he'll hurt Libi.

Before I can get much further, the idiot fists my hair, dragging me further into the room, chuckling as he sees Libi.

"See this bitch?" he snarls. "This is what happens when you don't do what you're told."

He lifts me by my hair, pain tearing at my scalp, my hands instinctively wrapping around his wrist to reduce the burn.

"Leave her alone!" Libi cries.

"Not until she pays," he snarls, dropping me to the floor.

I try to hold in my sob, seeing him bend in my peripheral, and I'm too late to react when I realise what he's doing.

With the syringe now in his hand, he leaps on me, forcing me to the floor in some sort of MMA grapple that I can't get out of, my head slamming to the concrete floor again. My dark rimmed vision finds Libi, and I see her more than I hear her as she screams, her little face red, her tears falling like a waterfall.

The biting sting of the needle pierces my skin in the bend of my elbow, and it's too late, he's found the vein and he's injecting the rest of the Spaceball straight in.

My free arm flails, and I can see Libi pointing to something on the floor. I don't know why I can't hear her, but as the first rush starts to wash through me, my hand connects with something familiar, and I pick it up.

I feel like I'm having an out of body experience as I swing it towards the guy, plunging it into the side of his neck. This isn't something I wanted Libi to see, but as his hold on me loosens, and the heat of his blood washes over me, I'm almost certain I feel a smile tugging at my lips.

There you go, Santa.

I slayed.

"On your six." Wes, aka Wildcard, says quietly, his hand on my shoulder as Ghost does his thing and picks the lock.

"Viper to Cipher, confirm phone jammer is active," I say low as I watch Ghost click the lock open.

"Copy that. Jammer is working. Calls to emergency services can't be made."

I smirk to myself at Cipher's confirmation that he knew why I was asking.

The last thing we need are cops getting notified while we are in the middle of this. We can deal with the fallout later. Right now, I need to get my girls back.

As soon as Ghost pushes the door open, my gun is raised and we are moving in.

"Heat signatures show one inside the bathroom, two moving around in the living room," Cipher's voice rumbles in my earpiece. "Three in the kitchen. Another three in a small room downstairs, although one is cooling. As well as a couple at the rear of the house. And there are five or six in the rear shed."

"Copy that," I whisper, my eyes scanning everything we

pass on our way up the passage, our steps barely audible as we go. "Bruiser and Doc, move in."

"Copy." Bruiser acknowledges as Wes, Ghost, and I near the cracked door leading into the kitchen.

I lift my hand in a stop gesture, and we still as we wait, our focus on the room we are about to enter, but our senses scanning our surroundings every second.

"Three. Two. Go."

At Bruiser's countdown, we burst into the kitchen as quietly as we can, taking the three Serpents by surprise as they bag and weigh cocaine.

I don't hesitate to pull the trigger, instantly killing the lanky looking Serpent that goes for his gun, while Bruiser coming in from the outside door takes out the guy bagging the drugs, and Wildcard puts two shots into the third guy's chest, but not before he fucking yells, alerting the house.

Pounding feet on the timber floors indicate the others in the house know something's up despite us using silencers, and as soon as Ghost goes to move out into the hall, bullets spray the doorway, splintering wood as we take cover.

Lowering to his haunches just inside the door, Ghost locks his gaze with me, pointing to his eyes, and then low in the direction of the shooter, before pointing to me and Wes and then in the other direction, up the hall.

I nod, knowing exactly what he means, and Wes and I get ourselves into position as Ghost holds his hand up before counting down silently by lowering each finger.

Three.

Two.

One.

Ghost throws himself low, out into the hallway, landing on his back as he sprays bullets in the other shooters' direction, and I don't even risk a glance that way as Wes and I dash up the passage to the living room with Bruiser on our tail.

Getting low on my haunches, I press my hand to the cracked door and push it open, bullets immediately spraying our way, but since they are aimed high, they don't hit their mark.

Leaping up, I shoot in the direction of the shooter as I dart into the room, taking cover behind a table as Wildcard follows.

"Who are you?!" a voice bellows from the small room off to the side.

"Step out and I'll tell you!" I call, and the moment I do, a huge, beefed-up guy leaps up from behind the couch and starts shooting in my direction.

He only gets two shots off before his head whips back, and a stunned look falls across his face as blood starts to pool from the hole now in his forehead thanks to Bruiser, before he tumbles to the floor with a loud thud.

Dashing out from behind the table, I train my gun on the door that the voice came from.

"Come out," I call. "You have nowhere else to go."

"Not until you tell me who the fuck you are!" the guy bellows, and given he was being protected by the now dead beefed-up guy, I'm gonna guess the Serpents leader is behind the door.

Snake.

"Cipher to Viper." Julian's voice crackles in my ear. "Send Ghost out and we'll check downstairs where the other heat signatures are."

My eyes dart to Colt, and I give him a nod before he glides out of the room with a level of silence that sends a chill up my spine.

"Want me to kick the door down?" Bruiser asks, and I consider it for a moment.

We have to assume Snake is armed, which means he'll have a direct line to shoot Bruiser. However, we've done this shit before, so I nod before locking eyes with Wildcard and gesture to Bruiser's left side.

With my best mate's eyes trained on me, I point to my hand, arm, and legs, and he nods, knowing I'm telling him to shoot Snake's limbs so he can't shoot at us, or try to run. Since Wes and I will have a different angle, my focus will be on the opposite hand, arm and leg as Wes.

This time it's me who does the silent countdown using my fingers, and the moment I get to one, Bruiser kicks the door with everything he has, and the fucking thing swings open, slamming wide.

Snake isn't in the doorway like we planned for, but the moment Bruiser's gun breaches the threshold, bullets from a semiautomatic spray the doorway.

Wes, being on the far side, gets hit, blood spraying from his arm, but the crazy fucker charges straight past Bruiser, into the small bathroom, pulling the trigger and hitting his target.

I'm expecting to walk in and see Snake with a bullet between his eyes, but Wes understood the fucking assignment, shooting at Snake's arms and one leg to render him fucking useless.

"Fuck, Wildcard. You okay?" I grin as I pass him, and he heaves through the pain of his flesh wounds as he nods.

"Any other job and the fucker would be dead," Wildcard snarls through gritted teeth, stepping back so I can deal with the prick that shot at us.

Dion Abraham. The Serpents' ruthless leader, better known as Snake.

"Where are they?" I snarl, and the fucker has the audacity to play dumb.

"Who exactly are you looking for?"

Lurching forward, I jam the barrel of my gun up under his chin, forcing his head back as he hisses in panic.

"You fucking know exactly who I mean. Your men kidnapped my daughter!"

When a menacing smile spreads his lips wide, revealing decaying teeth, I have to fight the urge to smash the butt of my gun against them.

"Kidnapping that little girl was not my order. Carlos did that all on his own, doing a favour for his whore of a cousin," Snake snaps at me, his lip curling in disdain. "He paid the price for that. With his life."

"So where the fuck is my little girl?" I jam the gun harder, relishing the hiss of pain that leaves his lips.

"She's my little girl now."

The moment those words leave his lips, something inside me fucking snaps, and I squeeze the trigger, painting the tiles with his brain.

19

BELL

I'm crushing Libi behind me, into the far corner as the pounding of more heavy feet come our way. The cocktail of drugs pumping through my veins is making it hard for me to focus on all the noises I hear, and I'm pretty sure I'm rocking a concussion, but I force my lids to stay open as I stare at the door, the blood coated knife tight in my grip, stretched out in front of me.

"Bell," Libi whimpers behind me, her small little hands clutching at the back of my dress as I hide her with my body again.

This feels like déjà vu.

"It'sss okayyy," I slur, my limbs feeling like they are wrapped in concrete.

That hit straight into my vein is severely messing with me. I'm fighting the pull to pass out, to let the drugs completely take over me. But I have to fight so I can protect Libi. I just have to.

Black booted feet suddenly come into view, attached to legs that seem to move so quietly compared to the herd of elephants storming in behind him.

"Stay back!" I screech, jutting the knife in their direction, but my words don't deter their approach.

"Bell. It's us," the familiar voice says, bringing tears to my eyes as I peer up and try to focus my gaze, but I'm met with a black and white mask, and I shrink back against Libi as I wave the knife around.

"I said, stay back!"

Libi's whimpers meet my ears, and all I want is to turn around and hug her and tell her that everything will be okay, but I can't. I have to protect her, to make sure these men can't get to her and do unspeakable things.

"Bell, it's me." The black-clad figure lowers to his haunches, one hand outstretched in a calming motion as the other reaches up and tugs off the mask.

I blink. And then blink again, this time more tears springing to my eyes.

"Ghost?" I whisper, seeing the familiar face of one of Kit's team members.

Is he really here?

"Yes." He nods. "You're safe now."

I shake my head, my eyes darting over his shoulder to the other black-clad men, their masks still in place.

"No, stay back!" I jab the knife towards him, and in a flash of movement, he snatches the blade from my sluggish grip.

I scream, and flail, trying to fight, but I'm no match for him, and before I realise what's happening, his strong hands are on me and I'm pinned under him to the cold concrete floor, and the only sound I can hear is Libi screaming.

20

KIT

The unmistakable scream of my little girl has me bolting through the house, down a short set of stairs and a long passage, slowing as I leap over a couple of dead bodies, noticing their throats slashed.

Shit. That's not my team's style.

"No!" Bell's voice meets my ears, spurring me forward. "Don't touch her! Leave her alone!"

I burst into the room, nearly slipping on a pool of blood with my gun raised, as Cipher and Doc whip off their masks, while Ghost pins Bell to the floor.

What the fuck…

I can't make fucking sense of things.

Taking a steadying breath, I try to analyse the scene.

Then my eyes land on the fragile, trembling form of my little girl, huddled in the corner, wielding a fucking knife.

"Libs!" I almost fucking cry, reaching up to tug off my mask so she can see it's me. "It's me, sweetie."

Those big doe eyes shoot up and lock with mine, fear bursting from them in the form of tears as her lower lip wobbles.

"D-daddy?"

I step further into the room, bending to lay my gun on the ground before raising my hands in front of me in a calming gesture.

"Yes, Libi. It's me. Daddy."

A sob lurches from her before she lets the bloody knife tumble to the floor and runs for me.

I meet her more than halfway, catching her as she leaps at me, her guttural cries nearly breaking me as I finally hold her in my arms.

"Shhh. It's okay. Daddy has you. You're safe now."

Her cries don't ease, her little arms so tight around my neck that it's entirely possible she might choke me out soon.

With my hands clutching her to my chest, I quickly study the space again, my gaze snapping to Ghost, who is no longer crushing Bell to the floor but is hovering over her as he speaks to her quietly.

The fuck happened down here?

"Is she alright?" I ask Ghost while Wildcard moves past me to lower to his haunches on Bell's other side.

"It's okay, Bell," he rasps, lifting her blood-soaked hand in his. "Libi is safe."

She mutters something I can't understand, which is when I notice her hand flop back against the floor with a thud and Wes darts a concerned gaze my way.

"She's taken a beating and... they drugged her."

Those three words have my heart sinking.

They drugged her.

The Serpents drugged Bell.

Bell, who is a recovering addict.

Bell, who had been sober for nine hundred and twenty days.

Fuck.

Standing, Ghost turns to me, but my eyes move past him to land on Bell, finally giving me a better look.

She's a mess. Her dress is torn. Her hair is a frazzled mess. Her eye makeup is smeared. And she's covered in blood.

"Has she been stabbed?" I snap, and Ghost shakes his head.

"Not her blood." He points to the dead body on the floor to our left and then to the door, indicating to the hallway.

Shit.

She did that. She killed those men for Libi. For me.

"I couldn't letttt..." Bell's slurred voice draws my attention, and she parts her lips to say more, but it's just mumbled babble.

"Daddy," Libi hiccup-sobs in my ear. "Bell saved me. She stopped the bad men."

I nod, rubbing her back. "I know, sweetie."

Fuck. I want to lift Bell in my arms too, but I can't for the life of me let go of my little girl right now, all the fear building in me since she was taken rushing to the surface... but I want to hold Bell too.

Fuck. I care about her more than I realised.

"Sant...a," Bell slurs, and immediately my eyes lock with her heavy-lidded gaze. "I slaye...d."

Fucking hell. Even as she stares death in the face she's still fucking around, and my team doesn't miss her words, their light snickers filling the space.

Standing from Bell's side, Wes moves to me, clapping me on the shoulder. "We'll take care of Bell, mate. You look after your little girl."

I nod, realising my emotions are clearly written across my expression, before I turn to Doc.

"She was nine hundred and twenty days sober until today. She's gonna need our help... your help." I clear the emotion starting to clog my throat, and Doc nods.

"We've got this, Viper." He reaches out and gives my arm a squeeze right as Bell's incoherent babble cuts off, and she starts to seize.

21

BELL

I feel like a caged animal as I stare at the bedroom door, yet I don't have the willpower to get off this bed and free myself.

I'm not a prisoner. Not even a patient. I'm free to step right out that door whenever I want. Yet I don't. I can't.

I just... can't.

My entire body aches, like I've been hit by a train and then run over by a long line of trucks in its wake.

I didn't ask for this. I didn't even go seeking it out. Yet the crash of those substances lighting up my veins has hit harder than I could ever imagine.

One instance. Not even a relapse but forced on me by a monster, and now I'm terrified the moment I walk out that door, my feet will lead me to find another hit.

The fatigue and tremors only lasted half a day, but the emotional crash is what's taking longer than I expected. I don't know if I'm strong enough to fight the urge if it hits me.

The way I felt with the cocaine in my system... It'd just be so easy to say, 'fuck it', and give in to the temptation.

But shit, I came close to it all ending, and if it wasn't for

Doc's quick response to my seizure, I'm not sure I'd be here today to dwell over everything.

I know it's only been a couple of days since it happened, but I need to get to a meeting, or call my sponsor or something.

The rap of knuckles against the door has me stiffening, and I'm about to call out that I don't want visitors when the door opens, and Kit's blue eyes find mine.

"You're awake."

I don't respond as he steps into the room. The guest room, I might add.

I guess I'm getting what I wanted in the first place. To be left alone. For me and Kit not to be a thing.

I don't say anything. I can't. My head isn't right. My emotions are up the shit. And I feel like a ticking time-bomb.

Moving across the space, his eyes rake over me, lingering on the side of my face where I know there are bruises. They match the ones on my back, where I was sure I might have broken something after what happened, but Doc cleared me with a cracked rib. Not a break.

According to him, I'm as tough as nails. I don't feel it though. Not today.

As Kit closes the distance, he holds something out to me, and my gaze falls on Christmas wrapping paper and a little red bow.

My brows shoot up as I glance back up at him.

"A gift. From Santa." He smirks, and shit, I can't even fight the way my lips start to spread wider in a grin.

"Sant..." I clear my throat and try again. "Santa?"

He nods, lowering to sit on the mattress by my side.

"Special delivery." He presses it into my hands, forcing me to take it.

"I don't have anything for you," I rasp, my mood

plummeting as this stupid fucking rollercoaster I'm on drops low again.

"Trust me, this gift is for both of us."

When I lock eyes with him, mine burn with the threat of tears, and he must notice, his own gaze softening.

"You're okay, Bell. Libi's okay. We are all okay."

"But Libi... Kit, she won't be okay. This will haunt her."

His eyes drop to my lap as he nods. "I know. I've already reached out to my therapist to get the details of one that can help her."

"You have a therapist?" I whisper, but he hears, those blue eyes flicking back up to mine as he nods.

"I do. I know Tillie would have told you what we both suffered through as kids. I work on that shit every fucking day to make sure I'm the best dad I can be for my little girl."

Shit. I don't know why that surprises me so much, but it does.

Kit can be a hard arse. He's not a feelings kind of guy, although, I must admit the way he's been with me has opened my eyes to a different version of him.

"Has Libi spoken much about what happened?" I ask, worrying my lip between my teeth for a moment. "I don't exactly remember much, but I remember her. I woke up to her little hand stroking my head, begging for me to wake up. She sounded so scared, Kitson. So bloody scared."

His eyes glass over with a wet sheen, revealing his vulnerability.

"Things could have been worse for her if you hadn't gone there, but fuck, Bell. What were you thinking?"

"I was thinking I'm some badass serial killer that lures predators in and kills them without too much drama." I shrug, cringing. "This time, I'll admit, I was in over my head."

His hand darts up to cup my face as he tugs me closer, his eyes wild.

"No fucking shit. They drugged you. Fuck, Bell. You could have been killed."

"I know," I breathe as he stares so deeply into my eyes that I swear he can see all of my secrets. "I would have happily died for her though. You know that, right?"

"I fucking know," he rasps, emotion clogging his throat before he presses his lips to mine.

I'm really not used to kissing so much. It's entirely possible I have a new addiction though, because kissing Kitson Hall is quickly replacing my need for breath play.

Shit. There are so many feelings rushing through me right now as our tongues brush. I feel like I can't get close enough, and I can hardly understand it since I really prefer space rather than human contact if I can help it.

When he breaks the kiss, all I can focus on is the threat of tears I'm not used to giving in to, and I force my eyes low, hoping he doesn't see.

"Hey." His fingers hook under my chin, lifting my head so I have no choice but to look at him. "I'm sorry you got dragged into all of this. And I'm really fucking sorry they drugged you. But I'm not sorry for the way I feel about you, Bell. Not one fucking bit. None of that has changed for me. If anything, the fact you willingly put yourself in danger to save my little girl has only solidified my feelings for you."

When I part my lips to speak, his finger presses to them, shushing me.

"Yes, Bell. I have feelings for you. Strong feelings. And yeah, I know they are largely tied to how well we match in the bedroom, but fuck, I can't deny that we are pretty fucking compatible out of it as well."

I shove his hand away so I can speak.

"We argue, Kitty Kat. A lot. That's hardly compatible."

He chuckles. "Actually, I think it makes us more compatible." He shuffles closer, reaching out to grip my hips, and a second later, he lifts me to straddle his lap, bringing us face to face. "Life would be boring if all we did was get along."

"Tillie…" I breathe as his fingers weave into my hair.

"Is fine with it."

My brows hitch. "You told her?"

"Fuck yeah, I did. She even lectured me for a full half an hour over the phone about disowning me if I break your heart."

"She did?" I whisper, feeling those raw fucking emotions again.

I figured I'd be the one who got lectured. Or cast aside. I'm not her blood. She owes me nothing, and I've probably brought Tillie more heartache than happiness over the years. I was sure she'd think I wasn't good enough for her brother.

"She did. Have you been teaching her about your serial killer ways?" he smirks teasingly. "I actually believed her when she said she'd chop my nuts from my body and grind them up in a blender."

A laugh bubbles from my lips, and the worry I'd been feeling starts to recede.

"That does sound like something I'd say."

He nods. "Exactly. So, you know how much I love my nuts. I'm not about to risk them on just anyone."

My gaze falls to his lips as the overwhelming urge to kiss him again starts to consume me.

"You'd risk your old man balls for me?"

"A thousand times over," he chuckles, shaking his head. "And they are *not* fucking old man balls. I'm only thirty."

"Yeah," I scoff. "Like I said, old man—"

Before I know what's happening, he growls and steers my head with his tight grip in my hair, smashing his lips into mine.

The moment our tongues brush again, I melt. I feel like putty in his hands. Completely and willingly at his mercy, and

I realise there's no other drug on this Earth that can make me feel like this.

Kitson Hall is it. My kryptonite. My addiction.

We moan into each other's mouths as I roll my hips, feeling his hard length bulging under the fabric of his shorts, right against the damp part of my panties.

"Fuck, Bellicent." Kit breathes against my lips, not willing to pull back completely. "The images those lips conjure in my head. I fucking love kissing you."

I can't help but deepen the kiss at his words, feeling like I'm more than I've ever been to anyone in these moments we share.

It's almost overwhelming, and before I realise what I'm doing, I pull back and slap his face.

His eyes flare and he hisses, fisting my hair tighter.

"You want to hurt?" he seethes, and I nod, desperate to feel him unleash his beast.

"Remind me why we are as compatible as you say we are," I sneer, and those kissable lips of his kick up at the corners.

"Did they touch you?" he snaps, and I quickly shake my head, knowing that he wants to know if they raped me, and his shoulders drop in relief.

I don't bother telling him about the blowie I gave Snake on the way to his house. I was playing a role. It was a necessity in order to find Libi, and some things, Kit just doesn't need to know.

"Fuck. That's good." He smiles, running his hands over my hair like I'm precious, and shit. I don't think I've ever been precious to anyone.

Always the one they want to fuck. Never the one they want to keep.

But Kit wants me. More than just to fuck, otherwise telling Tillie wouldn't have been necessary.

"I want to punish you, Bell. So fucking much, but first, open your gift from Santa."

I snicker, biting my lip as I ease back from him, my fingers already gripping the gold and black Christmas paper so tightly that I've made a hole in the wrapping.

Both of us cast our eyes to the gift, and I tear at it, eager to see what Kit got me.

The moment the paper is free, a laugh bubbles from my lips as I hold up the open mouth gag between us.

"Oh Santa. This is the best pressie I've ever gotten," I say dramatically, grinning at Kit, and he winks.

"Told you it was for both of us."

It's like he sees directly into my dirty soul, and I can't help but scoot forward and grind on his lap again.

"If you're going to punish me, get to it, Santa. Or I'll find a Grinch to do it instead."

His growl is deep as he stares at me.

"I'll give you whatever the fuck you want, but tonight, no fucking breath play. Your seizure scared the fuck outta me. I want you present and conscious through every bit of it."

I nod, feeling my cheeks flame at the reminder that not only did I have a seizure, but I puked. I don't remember any of it, but Colt filled me in on all the gory details when I asked him for the truth of what happened after I blacked out at the Serpent house.

I have no recollection of a number of hours afterwards when apparently Doc hooked me up to an IV and flushed my system, while also running bloodwork to see what the Serpent king had injected in my veins.

Cocaine, like I thought, laced with Fentanyl.

I nod willingly at Kit, not quite having the usual urge to chase the high of walking the line of death. I don't remember ever feeling like that. I've always been somewhat self-destructive after the day I killed my own father and then found my mother dead, and the day I attempted to take my life once when I was sixteen. But since then, I found a way to chase pleasure while seeking possible death, and now, the thought terrifies me.

"Is that a deal breaker?" Kit's words have me blinking, and I realise I zoned out.

"What?"

"No breath play tonight. Is that a deal breaker?"

"Oh... uhhh, no. That's not a deal breaker."

His blue gaze is analysing as he studies my expression, his big hands coming up to cup my jaw.

"You know you don't have to be strong all the time, right? I know I've been a prick to you for most of the time we've known each other, but I now know it's because I was fucking scared and confused by the way I felt around you. Fuck, just take a look at Rhonda. That stupid bitch is an ugly version of you. Just too short, too fucking selfish, and fucking coo-coo."

A laugh bursts from me. "You do know who you're talking to, right? You read my files, for Christ's sake. If anyone is coo-coo, it's me."

"Yeah-nah, fuck that." Kit grips my hips and flips us, my back slamming to the mattress as he grinds his hard cock between my legs. "You were a prisoner in your own home. Your dad was your mum's dad, for fuck's sake. He raped her daily. Beat her. Beat you. Kept you both isolated from the fucking world." He brushes some of my wayward dark strands back off my forehead, and I wrap my legs around his waist, loving the way he sets me alight, even as we discuss something so fucking heavy.

"I still killed him."

His lips spread wide.

"Yeah, you fucking did, Belladonna."

I roll my eyes, the name not stinging as much as usual, as

I let myself feel his praise. I've never felt proud of what I did, but it was necessary for my survival.

Kit's blue gaze is intense as he studies me, like he's seeing something for the first time, and then, he leans down, nipping at my lips.

"You killed him by growing Belladonna in the veggie patch and poisoning him. He didn't even fucking question what the seeds were for when you gave him the shopping list. That dumb fuck deserved to die, and the fact he had a hand in his own death is even fucking better. But don't you call yourself coo-coo for coming out the other side with battle scars, Bell." He runs his fingers down over my neck and chest where my tattoos cover the evidence of my childhood. "They may have played a part in the person you've had to become. But they don't define you."

"Stop," I whisper as tears pool in my eyes, but Kit shakes his head.

"I'll never stop reminding you that you are worth it."

"I'm a killer," I hiss through clenched teeth, feeling the burn of frustration at him dismissing the ugly parts of me.

"So am I," he presses his forehead to mine. "That's one of the reasons we are perfect for each other."

I snort. "You should be worried that I'll kill *you*, since you said I could if you get clingy."

"Nope." He nips at my lips while grinding his hard cock against my panties. "You won't kill me. You're just as addicted to this thing between us as I am. But fuck, I'd love to watch you do it."

He's right. I am addicted to this, and I'd never been interested in anyone getting clingy until now.

Until him.

Reaching between us, he frees his cock before hooking the fabric of my panties aside, and the moment the fat head of his dick presses against my folds, I part my legs wider, nearly forgetting what we are even talking about.

"You want to watch?" I ask breathlessly, surging up to urge his cock to enter me, and he teases my entrance, nudging the tip in a little.

"Fuck yeah. I wanna see how you seduce your prey, and then kill them." He pushes his hips forward, easing his tip in a little further. "I bet they don't even see it coming."

I moan as I grind against him, desperate to swallow his dick, my hands slapping to his ginger facial hair as my frustration sends me wild.

"They don't, which is why you should be scared, Kit. Because when you least expect it, I might just kill you."

He surges in then, both of us arching towards each other as the blissful pleasure our bodies make takes over.

There's no foreplay for this fuck, other than the words we shared, and if I let myself think about this too much, I might think we were doing that cringy thing people call making love.

We are making something alright, and while love on some level might be involved, what we are making is each other high.

"Fuuuck, Bell," Kit rasps, before leaning down to nip at my lips. "I'll never get enough of your cunt."

I whimper-moan at his words, losing myself to the feeling of being stretched by his dick while the bend in it hits me so fucking deep there's a flicker of pain. We surge towards one another, thrust after thrust, pounding, slapping, grunting with a feverous wildness that has my fingernails digging into his back until the warmth of his blood coats the tips, and we are crying out as we explode into our climax together.

There's just something about rippling around a cock while it thrusts inside you relentlessly.

Actually, scratch that. It can't be just any cock. It has to be Kit's.

Shit. It really is this man that is bringing me undone.

Teenage me would never have thought it possible.

What a silly bitch.

"Fuck, Bell." Kit pants, his weight heavy as he collapses on top of me. "I think the whole fucking house heard us."

I smile up at him in his dishevelled state, his auburn hair a mess, probably matching mine.

"Please tell me Libi isn't down the hall in her bedroom."

Kit shakes his head. "Nah. She's waiting for you in the living room. She has something to show you."

My brows shoot up. "She does?" I ask, shoving at his chest, but he doesn't move off me.

"She can wait." He nips at my lips again. "I needed to make sure you were feeling okay first."

"With your dick?" I snicker, and he chuckles, thrusting forward, which only makes his cum start to leak out around his cock.

"Wasn't my plan, but fuck, you have a way of riling me up." He eases out of me then, pushing off the bed to look between my legs. "Fuck, that's a beautiful sight."

I spread my legs wider like the filthy bitch I am, and squeeze my inner walls so more of his cum oozes out.

"Fucking stop it." He points sternly at me. "If you keep doing that, we'll never leave this fucking room."

"Do what?" I ask innocently, giving my inner walls another squeeze, and before I know it, a deep growl rumbles past his lips as he leaps on me.

22

KIT

Heavy rock Christmas music meets our ears as we descend the stairs, along with deep male laughter and the higher-pitched giggle of my Libi. The sound has warmth spreading through my chest, since this is the first time I've heard her giggle after getting her back from that Serpent fucker.

My little girl won't be the same. I fucking hate that thought. I know trauma all too well, and the idea that she feels so terrified all the time makes me want to kill again. But it's only been two days since it all happened. I need to give her time. We all just need some fucking time.

As we near the bottom of the stairs, my attention gets dragged back to Bell as she tries to pull her hand free from mine, her feet stalling as she stares at the entrance to the living room.

"I'm not letting you go," I remind her, and I wonder if she gets the double meaning to it.

"Libi doesn't need to see us holding hands," Bell whispers as she halts on the second bottom step.

Fuck. The bruising on the side of her face is darker today.

It's really fucking hard to look at, reminding me of her cracked rib.

Fuck. Was I too rough with her when I fucked her just before? Should I have even done that? What about her sobriety? Should I back off until she's seen a therapist?

I don't know the answers to any of this, and fuck, I'll do anything to help her, which includes keeping her safe. Here with me.

"Libi already knows that I like holding hands with you." I force my grin, and Bell's dark brows shoot up.

"You told her?"

"I did. I thought she should know why you will be sleeping in my room from now on."

This time, Bell rolls her eyes.

"I have my own room. You just fucked me in it."

Nodding, I lean close, bringing us nose to nose.

"I fucked you in the guest room, and since you are no longer a guest, you have to give that room up so a couple of my team members can crash in it."

As I ease back, a deep frown tugs at her brows, but before she can protest, Libi bounds out into the hall, spotting us.

"Bell! You're up! Come look!"

With one last slanted glare at me, Bell turns her attention to my daughter, shaking off my hand to take hers as she is dragged into the living room.

Following behind, I hear Bell gasp before she swings back to look at me.

"You found a black Christmas tree?"

"I did." I nod proudly. "And the guys found the perfect decorations to match Libi's instructions."

"Isn't it pretty?" Libi beams up at Bell before tugging on her hand to bring her closer. "See, there are little skeletons, and skulls, and black baubles…"

"You know, mate, she asked me to tell Santa to wear a black Santa suit next year."

My eyes snap up to where Wes is smirking next to me.

"A fucking black Santa suit? Where the hell am I going to get that?"

Wes chuckles. "Fucked if I know, but I told her Santa would *absolutely* do that, so you have a year to figure that shit out."

I knuckle punch his bandaged arm, and he hisses, holding his wound as his face turns red.

"Fucking uncalled for."

"Why would you tell her that?" I snap. "Now I'll need to find someone to fucking make it."

"Don't act like it's a bad fucking idea, mate." Wes smirks and wags his brows. "I bet Bell will enjoy the suit just as much... *Santa*."

I try to swing another punch at his arm, but he dodges it, cackling like a fucking idiot, right as the front door swings open.

"Did someone say it's Christmas?"

I don't look behind me at the sound of my sister's voice. I already knew she was coming. Instead, I keep my eyes trained on the two girls who have my heart.

Libi and Bell.

They spin with wide eyes, never looking more like mother and daughter, even though they aren't even related.

"Tillie!" Libi screeches over the thump of Spinal Tap's, Christmas with the Devil, while Bell's smile lights up her whole face.

I still don't look at my sister as Libi rushes past me to go to her aunt. I can't. The sight of Bell happy is just too stunning, even with the bruising on her temple.

As she steps closer, her dark eyes shift from Tillie and

Liberty's reunion to me, and even as that smile remains on her face, her brows shoot up.

"Aren't you going to say hi to your sister?" she asks quietly, but I shake my head.

"I'm too busy committing that beautiful smile to memory. Tills can wait."

Bell's face softens, and her cheeks flush red, and fuck, did I just make Bellicent Bishop blush, again?

"Stop," she whispers, drawing closer, but not close enough, so I quickly grab her, and gently tug her to my chest.

"I'll never stop loving you."

She snorts and rolls her eyes, trying to pull free, but I trap her against my chest, pressing my forehead to hers.

"Did you just fucking snort at me?"

"This thing between us has been a thing for like two minutes. You don't *love* me, Kit."

"You're wrong, Bell. We've known each other for years, and I now realise that I've loved you the whole fucking time. I was just too chickenshit to admit it."

Her plump lips part, but they snap shut again as she struggles to come up with a response.

"Do you know how many times I tried to get this to happen?" Tillie asks suddenly from beside us, and we both turn our heads to see my sister holding Libi in her arms, both of their smiles wide. "All the sleepovers. Me going to work an hour early when we were still in school, just so you two would be left alone, and you'd have to drive her places."

My brows shoot up at Tillie's admission. "I thought you said you'd de-ball me if—"

"What's de-ball mean?" Libi asks, and a giggle bursts from Tillie's lips.

"I don't know, Libs. Your dad says weird stuff sometimes."

Bell snorts again, and Libi nods.

"He says weird stuff aaallll the time," Libi agrees.

"Were you really snowed in?" Bell asks my sister, and Tillie sighs, easing Libi down off her hip.

"Yes. That was totally unplanned. But it seems like the universe wanted the two of you to realise you were made for each other just as much as me."

"It was Santa!" Libi screeches. "He must have gotten my letter. He gave me what I asked for."

Libi bounces excitedly on the spot, those big doe eyes bright as they jump between me and Bell.

"And what was that?" I ask my little girl, watching her smile grow.

"To bring me a new mummy that would make my daddy smile." She giggles and claps while jumping up and down. "He gave us Bell!"

Fuck... my cold black heart melts completely at Libi's words, and my gaze darts to Bell for her reaction, but nothing about the warm smile she offers my daughter tells me she's uncomfortable with the idea.

"I guess I'll have to thank Santa for that." Bell smirks, and Libi nods enthusiastically.

"Yes!" Libi cheers, clapping. "Santa loves hugs!"

I can't fucking help myself. I give Bell another gentle squeeze, making sure she can feel the growing bulge in my shorts as I press my lips to her ear.

"You can thank Santa by wearing the open mouth gag and letting him fuck that tight throat of yours again."

I'm expecting her to pull away and slap me, but she fucking leans in and nods against my ear.

"Did someone say lunch is ready?" Tillie suddenly bursts out, hurrying for the hallway dragging my daughter behind her, already knowing I'm about to kiss her best friend.

By the time I hear Libi giggling in the next room and the

heavy steps of my men following, I have my tongue in Bell's mouth as she sucks on it, and my hands fisted in her hair as we both fight for control.

We kiss for so long, the hard rod of my cock feels like the skin will split at any moment, but then Bell stops abruptly, her breathy voice drawing my attention.

"You planning on watching the whole event?"

Dragging my heavy lids open, I find Bell staring to the side at my best mate Wes sitting in the armchair, casually watching us dry hump up against the back of the couch.

"I'd rather join in."

Bell's brows shoot up, and I chuckle at their exchange.

"He's the one I said I'd share you with," I remind her, and those dark orbs flick back to me.

"I thought..."

When she frowns and stiffens in my arms, I realise I've fucked up. The only problem is I don't know how exactly.

"You thought what?"

"Never mind." She tries to pull away, but once again I keep her trapped in my arms.

"I do mind." I growl. "Very fucking much. Tell me."

For a long few beats, Bell just stares at me, and I swear I see a thousand different emotions flicker in her eyes. I should tell Wes to leave, but clearly this has something to do with him.

"Bell. Talk to me. Yell at me. Tell me what I've done wrong."

Her lips part as she shoots a look in Wes's direction before coming back to me.

"I thought you wanted to keep me," she whispers, and fuck, my heart cracks as it sinks.

"I fucking do."

"But you want to share me? That's normally stuff guys do before they ditch me. Tell a girl what they want to hear just to get what they want, and then leave, like her purpose has been met."

"Bellicent, fuck. That's not what's happening here. I thought you'd enjoy it. Being consumed by two guys at once. Two guys that you can trust completely. But we don't have to." I shake my head as I cup her face, hoping she hears the honesty in my voice. "I just want to make you happy."

She stares at me for a long moment, and even though her eyes glaze over, no tears fall.

"Happiness is a foreign concept to me."

Fuck if those words aren't heartbreaking.

"Not anymore, Bells."

"You fuckers are making me wanna off myself, not get hard. What sort of show is this?"

At the sound of Wes's voice, Bell finally relaxes, a slight smirk tugging at her lips.

"Do you like to watch?" she asks me, and fuck, I nod quickly. "Good. Give me a few more days to recover, and then I'll show you how I got the name, *The Seduction Slayer*."

My lips spread wide. "Deal. But if you call it my room, and not our room one more time, breath play is off the table for a month."

She gasps, shoving me back, and I stumble, my cock tenting my shorts.

"You wouldn't dare."

"I fucking would, and you know it." I rearrange my cock, ignoring the way Wes laughs at my expense. "It's *our* room. And this is *our* house."

"I live in Melbourne."

"Not anymore. Now you live here."

She rolls her eyes. "My work is in Melbourne."

I shrug. "There are predators that need killing in Sydney, Bell. A fucking lot of them."

"He's right." Wes stands from the armchair, pointing at Bell. "You're needed here. And not just to ride his face."

When Bell drags her gaze from my best mate back to me, I see the resolve wash over her even before she nods.

"Fine. I'll move here. I'll call this place mine, but under one condition."

"Anything," I agree, and her smirk turns sinister.

"Rhonda must die. That bitch of a woman doesn't deserve Libi. And she never fucking deserved you. Kill her, and we have a deal."

Wes chuckles, clapping me on the shoulder on the way past. "You may as well tell her now."

"Tell me what?" Bell snaps, her dark brows hitching.

"We killed the leader of the Serpents and some of his men two nights ago. We also discovered a handful of women in the back shed of the house he took you to. They were drugged up and being trafficked. My team put them into protective care where they will get the treatment they need to withdraw and recover, but that comes at a cost."

Cocking her hip, Bell wraps her arms over her chest. "Which is?"

"We owe them a blood debt. In order to stop a full-blown war igniting between us and them, I have agreed to hand over someone. The same someone that started all of this."

"Rhonda," Bell whispers, her arms falling to her sides. "Will they kill her?"

"Most likely. But they may do unthinkable things to her first."

Slowly, my woman smiles like the cat that got the fucking cream.

"Good. Because that man had plans for Libi. Unimaginable plans that we will *never* discuss." Bell's lip curls in disdain. "Any mother who can treat their child like a bargaining chip, putting them in unspeakable danger, deserves everything the Serpents will give her."

Fuck. I already know that, but the fact this woman before me feels the same way. So protective of a little girl that isn't her blood just reconfirms Bell is my fucking soulmate.

BELL

The glare Rhonda gives me has me blowing her a kiss as Wes drags her out of the back of a black van. She struggles against his vice-like grip, trying to get at me, snarling like a rabid dog as I continue to tease her just like I did during the whole drive here.

"Let me go!" Rhonda seethes, and Wes simply scoffs as she keeps fucking screeching. "My cousin and the Serpents are going to kill you all."

Oh Rhonda.

I roll my eyes at her dramatics.

The Red Belly Team had apparently seized her the moment she stepped foot out of lockup. I didn't know any of this until Wes mentioned picking up the bitch from their other location earlier today. They'd been keeping her locked away until she confessed to everything, only to turn around again and deny it. But she had admitted to everything. Calling her cousin and asking him to kidnap Libi with the intention of swapping her child for a bag of cash.

She deserves everything that's coming her way.

"How dare you treat me this way!" She flails in an attempt to get away, but Wes's grip on her is firm.

"You mean the way you treat other people?" I ask, and the bitch spits at me.

Thankfully, the few metres between us saves me from having to wear that filth.

"Shut the fuck up, Rhonda," Kit barks, jabbing a finger in her direction. "You've been treating people like shit for years. Using them for your own gain. Taking what you fucking need with no care about who you walk all over along the fucking way." Kit curls his lip and bares his teeth. "Not fucking anymore."

"Besides," Wes smiles down at Rhonda, "Carlos is dead, and so is the Serpent leader, because of you. So now they want someone to pay."

Even though the lighting on this rooftop is dull, I can see the way Rhonda pales.

"What do you mean?" Her frantic eyes dart from Wes to us, then to the group of Serpents waiting on the other side of the parking lot.

"He means you belong to the Serpents now. And what happens to you is up to them." I grin, slipping my arm around Kit's back as he pulls me to his side.

"Usually it's blood for blood," Kit adds. "But I wouldn't be surprised if they play with you for a bit. Make sure your last moments alive are spent wishing you'd chosen to be a decent human rather than a soul sucker."

"By the time they are done with you," I smile, loving the stunned fear on her face as she realises she fucked people over one too many times, "you'll be begging for death."

A strangled cry slips from her lips as she spins and tries to run, but she's met with a wall of men. The Red Belly Team.

Ghost, always the quiet one, simply shakes his head at her. Doc, the oldest of the team, curls his lip as he hisses at Rhonda. Bruiser cracks his knuckles and snarls, "Run. I dare you." And Cipher simply lifts his gun, pointing it directly at her.

"Start walking, Rhonda," Kit demands, and her tear-filled eyes dart to him.

"Please. Kit. We can work this out."

"No, we fucking can't!" he booms, releasing me and storming towards her. "You had your cousin drug and kidnap Libi in the middle of the fucking night! Your own fucking daughter! And what for? Because you wanted more money that I refuse to give you! Because your daughter has unique tastes that you haven't even tried to understand! Because you didn't get your fucking way, and it all blew up in your face, revealing what a cunt of a human you are!" He opens and closes his fists, like he's trying hard not to fucking swing them at her. "You used your own daughter. You put her in danger. She hasn't been able to sleep alone ever since, you fucking cunt!"

His fury is blinding as his hand whips out, wrapping around her throat, and fuck, I instantly feel jealous.

I want that hand around my throat.

But this isn't about pleasure. This is raw pain and hatred. And Rhonda deserves every second of what's to come.

With a wild, unhinged look in his eyes, Kit walks Rhonda backwards, holding her up by her throat when she stumbles, his destination clear.

He's taking her to the Serpents himself.

No one stops him. We all stand and watch as she flails and screams, and the Serpents close the gap to collect their payment.

For a moment, I glance around at the view from this rooftop with the city lights in the distance and wonder if we will be heard by locals down on the street.

I heard Cipher saying something about cameras going

dark and phone signals being jammed, but still, if the Serpents use guns, surely someone will hear.

I don't really know what I expected. Maybe that they would put her in their car and drive away to deal with her in private, but the moment they have their hands on her, the screams that rip from her are no longer laced with fear. They are nothing but agonising pain.

There, under the lamplight on the top floor of the parking garage, the Serpents close in around her using barbed wire wrapped bats to get their pound of flesh.

The sickening crunch of bones breaking is loud, and Rhonda's screams turn to deep rasping gargles as each Serpent takes payment for the death of their leader and their men.

Kit doesn't spare another look over his shoulder as he storms back towards us, his eyes on his men before they land on me.

No words need to be exchanged. We all simply pile into the van, Rhonda's screams getting drowned out by the rumble of the engine, and we drive away, leaving her to her fate.

Even if someone on the street hears her screams, by the time help arrives, it will be too late.

There's a slight tremble in Kit's hand as he weaves his fingers with mine in the back of the van, and the moment we lock eyes, he starts to relax.

"She can't hurt Libs anymore," he rasps, and I nod, reaching up to brush my fingers through his auburn hair.

"She can't hurt you anymore either," I whisper, and a smile tugs at his lips before he presses them to my forehead.

"Soooo…" Wes leans in close beside us. "About that threesome…"

I suck in my lips, trying to hide my smile, but it's dark in the back of the van, so I know they can't see.

"I dunno…" Kit rasps next to me before pressing his lips

to my ear. "What do you think, Bell? You want me to share you?"

Heat pools between my legs at the thought, and suddenly, Wes feels closer than he was before.

"I don't know, Kitty. Do you think you can handle another dick fucking me?"

He growls low, like the idea is a struggle, but I feel his nod as his palm starts travelling up my leg.

"Not gonna lie. It's gonna fucking sting, but for once, I want to feel the humiliation of it, so when it comes time to punish you," his fingers disappear under my dress and press to my damp panties, "it'll be fucking brutal."

I moan, my chest heaving, and even though Kit is the only one touching me, I feel the heat radiating off Wes on my other side.

"Fuck," Kit groans, tugging my panties aside and running his fingers through my folds. "You're so fucking wet. You really do want to be shared."

"How wet?" Wes asks, and I whimper as Kit pulls his hand away, leaving me needy.

"This wet." Kit lifts his hand towards Wes, and I watch, barely breathing as Kit offers his best mate his fingers coated in my slickness, and Wes leans forward and sucks them into his mouth, groaning around them.

"Fuck's sake." Bruiser leans forward from the seats behind us. "Unless you are inviting everyone to the fucking party, Kit, keep that shit to yourselves until you're behind closed fucking doors."

24

KIT

Lounging back in the chair beside my bed, I can't stop my fucking knee from jiggling as my mind goes over everything that happened over the last week. Even though I know the new Serpent leader made sure no traces of Rhonda were left behind on that rooftop, I still worry the cops will show up asking questions.

We have everything covered, and our contact inside the police department will give us a heads up if need be, but there's always a possibility we missed something given the day and age we live in and the advances in technology.

I guess that's just another reason why Cipher is so irreplaceable.

He's fucking good at what he does.

"You sure about this?"

My gaze flicks to Wes where he's sitting on the edge of my bed in nothing but his boxers.

"I'm sure." I smirk at his uneasiness, something he doesn't usually feel in situations like this, but I guess this time, it's different.

Bell's different.

My eyes flick to the bathroom door as it clicks open and

Bell steps out wearing a red satin robe. My cock instantly starts to wake, and my gaze shifts back to Wes as he stands from the bed, watching my girl approach.

Sharing a chick isn't a new concept between us. But sharing a chick I actually care about sure fucking is.

There's a part of me that wants to dick punch him for looking at her the way he is right now, but then there's the other part of me. The depraved part. The part that craves the forbidden. That craves things most are too scared to admit to another.

I want to feel the jealousy of watching Bell with another man. I want the humiliation of it, so when it comes to me claiming her tonight, it'll be all the more fucking brutal.

For her. Not for me.

For me, it'll be fucking sweet.

"You hungry, Wes?" she asks as she rounds the bed to the side we are on, and he nods, rearranging his already hard cock in his black boxers.

"Fucking famished," he admits, and I can't even help the low growl that rumbles in the back of my throat.

Mine.

"Ohhh." Bell's brows shoot up as her attention shifts to me. "Is that jealousy I hear?"

"Punishing you is going to be a fucking pleasure, *Belladonna.*"

Her eyes flare at the name I know she hates.

I'm the only one that knows it's the name of the poison she used to kill her father, and only I can call her that and remain breathing.

It's our thing.

"Just for calling me that, I'm gonna make Wes fuck me longer."

"Fuck. No complaints here." He chuckles, but my eyes narrow, remaining on my woman.

I've delayed this from happening for a few days, making sure Doc checked over her first to ensure she's healing okay. While I don't intend on throwing her around tonight, I have no doubt things will get a little rough at some point.

"Do you have it?" I ask, and she nods, her gaze flicking to Wes as she pulls a long and thick butt plug from her gown pocket.

"Be a good boy and lather it up for me." She winks as she holds it out between us, and I pick up the lube off the bedside table and smear the fucking plug with the clear gel, letting it ooze down over her fingers.

Licking her lips, she holds the plug out to me, and I take it before she removes the red gown, revealing her full nudity other than the red heels she's wearing.

With the satin pooling around her feet, she turns, giving me her back, and my gaze instantly finds the yellowing bruises on the back of her ribs as she widens her stance and bends in half, pointing her arse in my face.

"Plug me up, Kitty. Make sure it's nice and deep."

The moment she reaches around to grip each of her arse cheeks and pulls on them to open her puckered hole up to me, I forget about the bruises and Wes groans, quickly shucking off his boxers and wrapping his hand around his cock as he starts to jack off.

Impatient fucker.

Shifting forward on the seat, I press the tip of the oversized plug to her puckered rose, and gently ease it in. Bell pushes back against me, like she's already desperate to be filled, and I insert it all the way in until all that can be seen is the red jewel.

"That feel good, Bell?" I ask, my voice a little huskier than it was a few minutes ago.

"So good it almost hurts." She breathes, straightening

before peering down at me over her shoulder. "You really want me to show you how I do it?"

I grin, nodding, fucking pumped to see what The Seduction Slayer does to her victims.

"How far?" she asks, and I shrug.

"Until I tell you to stop."

"How far, what?" Wes asks, none the wiser to the fact I've asked Bell to show me how she seduces and kills her prey.

Turning to face me with her hands on her hips, Bell ignores Wes, quirking a brow at me.

"What if it goes too far?"

My cock fucking jerks at the prospect.

Maybe we should have found a real victim, because I really want to see her kill. Fuck. I've never wanted anything more.

My gaze flicks to Wes, who seems to have forgotten about his question, his eyes trained on the jewel protruding from Bell's arse as he pumps his dick.

Maybe he should die for wanting her like he does.

"Keep going until I tell you to stop," I demand. "And not a fucking second before."

Bell's nostrils flare, and she nods, spinning away from me and pointing to the floor.

"Kneel."

Fuck. She's a switch. Dominant right now, and Wes doesn't even question it, the sadomasochist in him quickly adapting to the situation as he drops to his knees before my temptress.

"Can I get a kiss first?" he asks, but she shakes her head.

"My kisses are only for Kitty Kat." Her dark gaze flicks to me, a smile playing at the corners of those lush plump lips. "The only things you can put in my mouth are your fingers or your cock." She shifts her eyes back to Wes, and he nods.

"My cock is ready when you are." He gives it a pump from

where he's kneeling on the floor, and her eyes narrow into a glare.

"Touch your cock without permission again, and I'll put a cage on it."

It's almost laughable the way Wes holds his hands up like a gun is pointed at him.

"I'm at your mercy. Do with me as you please."

I bite back my laugh at my too keen best mate, but the moment Bell steps forward, fisting her claw tipped fingers into his hair, I stiffen.

"You're going to eat my cunt like a man starved," she tells him, jerking his head back to loom over him. "I'm well hydrated, Wes. So if I'm not drowning you in a fucking waterfall when I come, then you haven't done your job properly, and that cage is going on."

"Oh, fuck, yeah," he laughs, ever the cocky bastard. "Fucking smother me."

And she does.

With the curl of her lip, she shuffles closer until Wes's mouth and nose disappear between her legs, and my woman starts grinding against his face, her hand still locked in his hair.

When her dark orbs flick back to mine, I shift restlessly, my cock straining in my boxers as she watches me watching her fuck my best mate's face.

"How does this make you feel?" she asks, and a deep growl rumbles in my chest, causing her to smirk. "Fuuuuuck, Wes has a long tongue."

She emphasises that by dropping her head back as her pleasure builds, grinding her cunt faster against his face.

"Fuck me with that tongue, Wes," she demands, and the sloppy sounds of my mate's tongue diving inside her has me gripping the arms of the chair with force. "Oh yeah. Just like that."

I shift forward in the chair, wanting nothing more than to stop what's happening, but fuck, the fury I feel has my heart pumping in my chest, and I force myself to remain seated, letting her fucking edge me without even touching me.

With every grind and thrust, I can tell she's getting closer, and the moment she widens her stance and holds his head to her while she quite brutally fucks his face, I know she's about to come.

"Do it!" I yell. "Fucking drown him!"

She cries out at my demand, the spray of her orgasm washing over his nose, eyes and forehead as she jerks through each ripple, not letting him come up for air until she's done.

Fuck.

FUCK.

I'm harder than I've ever been, and I get the feeling that what she just did isn't part of what she normally does to seduce her victims. I'm pretty sure she did that just to rile me up.

And fuck. It worked.

A loud heave comes from Wes as she releases his head, my best mate sucking in much needed air as my woman starts rubbing the pads of her claw-tipped fingers over her clit, flicking the remnants of her spray over his face.

She's a fucking queen.

"Since you didn't touch your cock, you can fuck me now. Wrap it up and get on the bed."

My heart flips uneasily in my chest at the thought of him putting his cock inside her.

Mine.

While Wes rolls on a condom, Bell approaches me, reaching out to press her fingers to my lips.

"Open," she whispers, and I do, letting her sink two in, her sweet nectar bursting on my tongue. "Some men act like they want to be in control, but a lot secretly want a woman to take control and use them. Be at their mercy." She pops her fingers free. "Your mate is one of those."

"Am I?" I ask, already knowing the answer, and she shakes her head.

"No. And if he had been the one to manhandle me, you would have stopped this already."

I smirk, loving how she already knows me so well.

"It's still a fucking struggle," I admit, and she nods.

"Tell me to stop, and I will."

"Not yet." I growl, and she takes a step back, even as she whispers.

"Do you secretly want me to kill him? Because when I strike, I go for the kill, Kitty. Not to wound."

I fully recognise that my best mate's life is on the line right now. But the thing is, if I told him what was happening, he wouldn't stop this. In some ways, he's just as self-destructive as Bell.

"Don't stop until I tell you to," I demand, and she nods, biting her lower lip as she backs away, before turning to Wes, who has now positioned himself on the bed, his cock wrapped and ready to fuck.

25

BELL

There's no going back now. Kit seems determined to see this through, and while it's hot as hell to have his eyes on me while I'm like this, I worry about the aftermath.

Like, what happens if he doesn't stop me in time, and I actually kill Wes?

I'd like to think I won't do it, but I know myself. I know how I get when I get into that headspace. I have one goal. Seduce. Fuck. Kill. In that order.

The seduction part was easy since I didn't even have to do anything. So now it's time for me to fuck, which is the distraction phase of my work.

When a guy is buried to the hilt in pussy, close to coming, their head is nowhere else. It's the perfect time to catch them by surprise. Sometimes I even let them come and ride the last waves before I strike.

That's what I'll have to do tonight, but hopefully, Kit will stop me in time.

But what if he doesn't?

Climbing over Wes, his hands come to my hips as I straddle him, making sure we are in a position that Kit can see our faces, but also, so he can lean to the side to see his best mate's cock going in and out of me.

"You wanna fuck me, Wes?"

"Fuck yes. Is lover boy joining us?" he asks, and I glance over my shoulder at Kit who has a death grip on the arms of the chair.

"Soon." I smirk, bringing my gaze back to Wes. "He wants to watch me fuck you first. Would you like that?"

"Fuck yes." Wes nods, so I reach between us, lifting myself enough to line up his girthy cock, and slowly, I sink down.

There are three sets of groans as I seat myself, and when I glance back over at Kit, I see him taking his cock out of his boxers and fisting it, pumping it from hilt to bended tip.

I take it slow at first, rolling my hips, letting the girth of Wes's cock stretch me out while the plug in my arse makes everything feel so much tighter. Fuller.

I quickly realise that Wes is good at sex. Not just by the rhythm he keeps or the way he punches his hips right before he sinks all the way in, but by how long he seems to last. He's in no hurry. He likes making it last, which is both good and bad.

Good, because it feels fucking fantastic to have him fuck me while Kit watches, but bad because I'm desperate for Kit to join us, and the longer Wes lasts, the more drawn out my killing phase has to be.

"Does he feel good?" Kit asks from his chair, his voice husky and strained.

Nodding, I cup my tits as I grind down on Wes, letting my head fall back.

"So good."

"Better than me?" Kit growls, and heat flares over my skin at the possessive sound.

The answer is no, and I'm trying not to analyse why that

is. Kit's cock isn't a magical wand, but it belongs to him, so it may as well be, and that's what's throwing me.

I've only ever liked guys or girls because of the way they make me feel in the bedroom, but with Kit, it's more than that. So much more.

"Yes," I lie. "His cock is thick. Stretches me sooo good."

I hear Kit's growl, but don't look his way since I think that's what he wants.

"I don't think I'll ever have enough of it."

My lie is answered with the smash of a glass hitting the far wall, and I smirk down at Wes as worry pinches his brows.

"Maybe we should stop."

"No." I shake my head. "Kit wanted this. He can pay the price of knowing how much I crave his best friend's cock."

My words have a ripple effect.

Wes speeds up his pace, the words working like he has a fucking death wish, and I realise he's more like me than I knew, and he sits up, wrapping his arms around me as he tries to take control, pistoning into me from underneath.

Meanwhile, the chair Kit was in, is now lying in a broken heap over by the door, and I can hear and feel him pacing beside the bed as I force Wes's face between my tits and drop my head back, moaning.

"So good!"

Another growl from beside us, and I glance to the side to see Kit, fury contorting his expression as his fists ball tightly at his sides like he's considering lashing out.

"Tell me to stop." I breathe, and he shakes his head.

"Show me."

I think he actually wants me to kill his best mate, but if that's what he wants, then I'll give it to him. I won't even ask why.

As Wes and I fuck each other at a fevered pace, I reach to

the side, to the back of my red heels, and flip the small clip underneath, releasing the knife.

Kit watches everything I do, his eyes flaring wide and wild as I bring the knife around behind Wes.

With a simple lift of my brow, I silently wait for Kit to stop me, but he doesn't, so I accept that this is what he wants, and line the blade up at the back of Wes's neck, being careful not to press it against him so I don't alert him to what's about to happen.

The moment I move to press the tip of my blade to his skin, Kit's hand wraps around my wrist in a death grip, stopping me, and our eyes meet as he slowly, and carefully pries my fingers open, relieving me of the knife as he shakes his head and mouths, "Stop."

Meanwhile, Wes is none the wiser, still punching up into my pussy, and a level of relief I didn't expect to feel washes over me.

I really thought he wasn't going to stop me.

"My turn," Kit rasps, having slipped the blade into the drawer, and now climbing on the bed behind me.

"Fuck," Wes pants. "About time. I was about to nut."

Kit chuckles, the brush of his fingers grazing my arse as he tugs on the butt plug, slowly easing it out.

With the heat of his breath fanning my ear, his voice is quiet as he speaks.

"Enjoy this, Bell. This is the last time you'll ever be the filling in a sandwich."

Then he presses his cock to my arse, not covered in a condom like his best mate's, and he slowly squeezes himself in.

I can tell by the way Wes stops thrusting and waits for Kit to seat himself that they have done this before. Shared a woman.

I'm not too proud to admit that it makes me jealous.

"Kitty," I breathe, and he and Wes slowly start fucking me, consuming me completely from both sides.

"Yes, Belladonna." He nips at my ear, and Wes chuckles, obviously having picked up on how much I hate that name.

"You'd better enjoy this too, because this is the last time you share a chick with Wes or anyone else for that matter."

Wes roars with laughter, and Kit wraps me in his embrace, bringing his hand up to wrap around my throat from behind.

"Deal. Because from now on. You're mine, and *only* mine."

A whimper escapes me at his words, his grip squeezing my neck a little, even though he said he was going to deny me breath play.

I feel so full, pleasure hitting me from multiple directions as they both fuck me, and all I can do is hold on.

"Wes," Kit barks. "Bite her nipple."

My heart flutters with anticipation at Kit's order, and Wes chuckles, his hand instantly finding my tit and lifting it as his tongue flicks my piercing.

And then he bites. Hard.

At the same time, Kit squeezes my neck, and they both piston into me with sharp punches, which sends me skyrocketing in seconds.

A silent scream scratches my throat as I squeeze my eyes tight, blinding pleasure erupting inside me as wave after wave hits unforgivingly.

A few moments later, Wes releases my nipple as he throws his head back in a roar, and the combination of orgasms helps Kit get over the line, his pulsing cock matching his own groans as he fills my arse with cum.

I feel like I'm floating as our bodies slacken and slump against each other, Wes burying his head in my chest, and Kit in the crook of my neck.

This should feel weird, but it really doesn't.

I don't know Wes very well, but I know Kit. He obviously trusts Wes more than any other, and even though what we just did might seem weird to some couples, to me, it doesn't.

Kit trusts me and Wes enough to know that this was nothing more than sex.

I don't have the sort of feelings for Wes that I do for Kit. They are not even remotely similar. In fact, I'm not even that attracted to Wes. What I am attracted to is the way Kit makes me feel when he's watching me, and even though I'm glad they are on the same page about sharing, I will miss that feeling of being watched by him.

But I suppose there are other ways we can still have that.

Like self-play.

Or maybe even bringing him with me when I go to kill.

The guys ease out of me, and I wait for the pain of my ribs to hit, but it doesn't, my entire body still floating.

Moving to the end of the bed, I smirk over my shoulder at them before bending over and parting my cheeks, making a show of squeezing Kit's cum from my arse.

"Fuck, man. You've won the jackpot," Wes mutters, leaning forward to get a better look.

"Yeah," Kit smirks lazily, his eyes meeting mine as he relaxes back against the pillows. "I really fucking have."

"You feeling hungry, Wes?" I ask, and in unison, both of their brows hitch. "You wanna eat Kit's cum from my arse?"

I don't miss the excited flare in Kit's eyes as he sits up a little on the pillows, and Wes flicks his gaze to his best mate.

"Since this is our last rodeo, I wouldn't mind tasting your cum."

Oh helllll, the flush that washes over me at that admission takes me by surprise, and the moment Kit nods, fisting his best mate's hair and steering him towards me, I feel my pussy growing slick all over again.

We all shift around to get in position. Wes lying, me on my

knees as I hover over his head, and Kit getting the best view behind me.

"Feed him, Bell," Kit orders, and I part my cheeks again, bending closer as I clench my muscles and feel his seed oozing from my back passage.

Wes moans, the flick of his long tongue dragging over my arse, lapping at every last drop.

"Fuuuck. That's so fucking filthy." Kit stands from the bed, rounding the end to pace as he watches me. "You're such a filthy whore, Bell."

I grin wickedly, nodding. "I am, Kitty. *So* filthy."

Kit's jaw ticks, and I think perhaps he's finally at his limit of sharing me.

His blue eyes snap from me to his best mate, and when he speaks, the rasp in his tone is more animalistic than I've ever heard.

"Time to fuck off, Wes. I need to punish my woman."

My bedroom door clicks shut as Wes leaves me and Bell alone, and I can't fucking hold back the violence that's been building in me all fucking night.

Bell's eyes are on me, her head tilting in that way of hers as she studies me, clearly assessing how far she can fucking push.

"Lay down." I point to the bed, storming past it to step into my bathroom.

Bell's scoff meets my ears as I flick the shower on, the brat in her fuelling the need to hurt as it builds inside me.

Lathering up my cock with soap, I focus on getting it clean, before rinsing off the suds and barely drying myself, too fucking eager as I step back into my room.

Bell is on the bed, laying on her front, her head resting in her hands as she fucking kicks around those red heels like she's a little fucking brat.

And fuck, she is.

"On your back."

She doesn't move straight away, a shit-eating-smirk

playing at the corners of her mouth, but when the rumble of my growl meets her ears, she rolls her eyes and turns over to her back.

Reaching out, I grip her shoulders and manoeuvre her until she's laying sideways on the bed, her head tipped back over the edge.

Turning to the mirror behind me, I can see that she can see herself, and I nod, happy with the position.

"Make sure you watch." I point to our reflection. "See what you look like when I punish you for fucking my best mate."

Again, she rolls her eyes. "Please. I think you two really wanted to fuck. Were you thinking about his arse when you fucked mine?"

There's a teasing edge to her tone. One I'm going to fucking enjoy destroying.

"Maybe I did," I snap, ready to piss her off. "I especially loved how good his cock felt rubbing against mine as we both used you."

Her nostrils flare, and I chuckle, scooping up the gift I gave her for Christmas. When I glance back down, she looks ready to kill me, and fuck, maybe I shouldn't be poking the serial killer.

Nah. Fuck that. This is us. This is what we do. Rile each other up.

Bell doesn't speak as I fit the open mouth gag onto her, loving the look of the huge red silicone lips that spread her lips impossibly wide. Her sneering gaze doesn't leave me though. Not for one moment.

"That feel okay?"

"*Maw*." She tries to speak, and I snicker.

"What was that? I couldn't quite make out what you said."

Her eyes turn to slits, and she lifts her hand and flips me off.

"Looks like my brat is ready." I chuckle, reaching under the bed for the oversized bowl I put there earlier, and positioning it on the floor under her head. "Just in case you puke." I tell her. "I'm feeling pretty fucking violent. I might not be able to stop."

Again, she flips me off. But she doesn't shake her head. Doesn't sit up and try to get away. She stays in place and starts cupping her tits, rolling those fucking hard nipples between her fingers before tugging at the piercings.

"You're such a fucking tease," I hiss, my hand moving to my hard cock, giving it a few long pumps.

Fuck. This chick. I'm constantly hard around her. I don't think I'll ever get enough.

I don't wait any longer. I position myself at the edge of the bed, my stance wide, and I feed my cock into her open mouth.

"Fuuuck," I hiss, not allowing her a single moment to adjust to my intrusion, looking down at her throat to see my cock move under her skin.

Her stomach immediately curls inward as she gags around my length, but I ignore the way her body is protesting, because it's just a reflex, and I'll only stop if she wants me to.

Slowly, I start to fuck her throat, my hand hooking under the back of her head to hold her in just the right position to spear her nice and fucking deep, and I watch as her fingers move to her clit, circling and mashing her needy little bud as she lets me abuse her.

I'm not sure how she's gonna feel when I suggest couples therapy. I'm pretty fucking sure we both should address these dangerous fucking tendencies we have. Mine to hurt. Hers to feel abused. But I want this to fucking work. And I've never wanted anything to work with a female before, so I know she's it for me.

I just want to make sure we don't fucking kill each other.

Maybe only *nearly* kill each other.

I growl at that thought, the rage in me rushing to the surface as I picture Wes on this bed fucking her. The way she pressed his head into her tits and dropped her head back like she was loving it.

"Fuck, Bell!" I piston faster, hearing her gag over and over, and ignoring the gargles of her stomach attempting to expel. "This body belongs to me!"

Even with the lust and rage coursing through me, I hear her moan, her fingers mashing over her cunt faster. There's no need for me to pull out and give her a breather, because I'm ready to come now, and I can see she is too.

"Mash that clit!" I demand. "Squirt for me!"

She moves her fingers faster, even as her body locks up in another gag, and the second I see the first drop shoot from her cunt, I lean down, shoving her fingers away to latch my lips over her clit.

I suck hard, the swollen nub clearly sensitive given the way she jerks, and she drenches me. I slam my cock brutally down her throat in the best fucking sixty-niner I've ever had, and my cum bursts from my tip in a violent explosion.

It feels like I nut for fucking minutes with the way the intoxicating pleasure seems to go on and on, but I know it's only seconds. The best fucking seconds I've had in a long time.

When the ripples of pleasure subside, I release her clit, shifting up and easing my cock from her throat, and she quickly spins over, giving in to her body's reflexes, and coughing up my cum.

"Fuck," I pant, standing over her as she heaves to catch her breath, cum and drool hanging from her pried open lips. "I should make you drink that."

I'm joking of course, but the fact she shrugs at me, like

she would if I asked her to, has every violent ripple falling away like I've just shed my skin.

She really would give me anything.

I just hope the sadist in me is enough for the masochist in her.

BELL

Taking some time to clean up, I stay in the bathroom for longer than I should, needing a moment to wrap my head around everything that's happened lately, and what just transpired in that bedroom.

I don't feel weird about it, but it felt like the end of something between Kit and Wes, and the start of something between me and Kit.

I don't want to come between them, but the jealousy I felt earlier was real.

I'm not sharing him. And he declared that my body is his, so hopefully we are on the same page about that.

Shit. Have I finally found a guy that wants to keep me?

A few days ago, I came here to spend Christmas with my best friend and her niece, with the dread of having to endure her brother. The brother who hated me.

Now, everything has changed. He matched me in the bedroom. I risked everything for his kid. We killed for each other. And he wants me to stay.

It seems absurd to move here just like that, but here's the thing I've come to realise.

Kit and I have always been more. We just couldn't get past our own insecurities to see it.

Tillie obviously saw it. Libi is fine with it. So now I have to accept it. I have to let myself feel that thing I never thought I could have.

Happiness.

I'm wary, though. Not because of Kit. Even though this is new between us, it feels very real. Very right. But there's this pit of dread in my gut that I can't seem to shake. I know exactly what it is, and it's something I typically work on by myself, but for the first time ever, I don't want to do this alone.

I don't *have* to do it alone.

Clearing the lump in my throat, I tighten the satin robe around me and step out into the bedroom. Kit is on the bed wearing only his boxers, a tray of cheese, crackers and fruit beside him as he pops a grape into his mouth.

"Everything okay?" he asks, and I nod, but then shake my head.

Immediately his frown appears, and he sits up.

"You're not leaving, Bell. It's an argument you won't win."

My lips spread into a smile, something I know I've been doing so much more of since coming here only days ago. I could tease Kit a little and make him think this new arrangement is what's concerning me, but for once, I just want to be real with him.

Vulnerable.

So, I steel myself, and tell him the truth.

"I've already surrendered to that," I admit, enjoying the way his shoulders drop in relief.

"Then what's wrong? Was sharing you too much?"

I shake my head quickly. "No, it's not that either."

"Get that hot arse over here and tell me what's going on in that head of yours?" He pats the mattress beside him, and I have to clear the lump building in my throat as I gear up to open my heart.

Crawling up beside him, I make sure I'm angled his way so he can see my face, but I can't for the life of me look him in the eyes right now.

I can be open and honest and uncomfortably blunt about sex, filth, and murder, yet the real stuff... emotions... that shit is hard.

Still. I've never wanted to share this part of me with anyone before... until now.

"Nine hundred and twenty days."

That's all I need to say before he's pulling me to straddle his lap, those strong hands cupping my face as he forces me to look at him.

"I know. I'm so sorry, Bell."

A tear slips free, and it's something I'm not used to doing, ever, let alone in front of someone else. But here with him, I feel safe, so I let them fall.

"I'm on day three now, but... will you help me... help me get back to nine hundred and twenty days, and beyond? I'll need to go to meetings. Find a local sponsor. Maybe even therapy."

"Fuck yes." He presses his forehead to mine, our noses squishing together. "I'll do *anything* for you. In fact, I should let you know I'm also on day three."

My brows shoot up and I pull back to stare at him. "What do you mean?"

"I don't do drugs, but I do drink more often than I should. So, I decided that your day one was going to be my day one too. In fact, in case you didn't notice, there wasn't a drop of alcohol consumed at Christmas lunch."

My brows hitch as I go over everything in my head. There were jugs of juice. Water. Cans of soft drinks, but no... no alcohol.

"Kit. You don't have to do that for me. This is your house. You should be able to have a drink if you want one."

"Correction, this is *our* house, and I don't *want* or *need* one. And God fucking knows my team needs to lay off it."

I smile at that. "Well, if you change your mind, just know I'll be okay with it. Cocaine maybe not so much, so please refrain from that, but grog should be okay."

Kit chuckles. "I'll have none of that in *our* house, or around Libi." He gives me a squeeze. "So, day three we are."

"Day three we are," I agree, blinking at him as a warm smile washes over his features.

"Fuck." He reaches around, weaving his fingers into the hair at my nape, and tugs me close. "I'll never get enough of you."

He closes the gap, claiming my lips in a searing kiss, and I melt against him, loving the way his tongue has the power to unravel me as much as his words.

When we pull apart, we are a little breathless, but my stomach takes that moment to growl, and we both laugh before Kit lifts me off him, back onto the bed, and pulls the tray closer.

"Eat."

Smiling, I pick at some of the food, trying to ignore the fact I can feel Kit watching me.

"So, you'll stay then?"

I nod.

"Here. With me?"

I nod again, this time flicking my gaze to his.

"Just to be clear," he rasps, stabbing a finger towards me. "I'm asking you to be mine."

My lips kick up. "Yours to abuse?"

"Yes," he smirks.

"Yours to get rough with?"

"Absolutely."

"Yours to be shared?"

"No... Not again," he growls, running his hand through his auburn hair, leaving it a mess on top.

"Ditto." I grin, and before I know what's happening, his hands are engulfing my face again as he steals another searing kiss that finishes with a nip at my lips.

"Mmmm." He moans, his blue gaze lust drunk as he licks his lips. "Strawberry."

A laugh bubbles from me, and he shuts me up by tossing another bite sized chunk of strawberry in my mouth.

"You know that four letter word that starts with L and ends with E?" he asks, and my brows shoot up as I nearly choke on the fruit in my mouth. "I wanna say that to you without freaking you out again."

"Oh... you mean lube?" I ask and immediately laugh at his frown as I slap my hand over my heart. "Oh my gosh, Kitty. Do you lube me?"

Kit throws his head back laughing, even as he fists my hair and drags me closer again. "I fucking *love* you."

Shit... he really said it.

Again.

It all seems too fast, but then again, if I'm being honest with myself, we've been dancing around this for years. This pull we have. No wonder we've always been at each other's throats. We were both too scared to admit the truth.

That we cared for each other.

I don't know that I'm ready to say that I love him despite feeling it, but I respond in the only way I know how.

"I lube you, too."

A loud laugh bursts from him again, as the door bangs open and little feet run in.

"What's lube?" Libi asks, leaping onto the bed with us, and Kit quickly tugs a pillow from behind him to put over his boxers.

"Never mind." He rushes out as Tillie's head pops through the open doorway.

"Sorry. She got away from me."

I smirk even as Kit glares at his sister.

"Is lube a swear word like dick?" Libi asks innocently. "Because Tillie said Wes was being a dick for telling the others about the bedroom games you played, but she won't give me two dollars to put in the swear jar."

"Libi, you can't say dick," Kit barks, and her little face morphs into a frown.

"Why? Tillie said it."

"Well, Tillie is in trouble." Kit glares at his sister, who just rolls her eyes.

"You said it too, Daddy. Just now when you told me I can't say dick."

I can't even remotely control the laugh that bursts from me, and Tillie slaps her hand over her mouth as Kit groans.

"Well, from now on no one can say that word," he snaps, and Libi nods enthusiastically before leaping back off the bed and running out the door.

"No one is allowed to say the word dick from now on! Daddy said so!"

"For fuck's sake. Why isn't she in bed?" Kit grumbles as Tillie laughs, not even able to speak as she closes the door and goes after Libi, who is making sure everyone in the house is aware of the rules.

"I swear, that kid will be the death of me."

"Nawww." I pout on Kit's behalf, reaching out to grip his short bearded jaw and squish his lips as I give it a squeeze.

"If I say the word *dick* around Libi, will *Santa* punish me?"

Kit's lips spread into a wicked grin. "Santa will punish you so fucking good."

I bite my lip. "I want Santa to punish me now."

"Now?" Kit's brows lift. "You want Santa's fist again?"

I nod, eagerly. "So much."

"Start lathering up that cunt with lube while I slip on the suit," he growls, and I don't hesitate for a second, excited for this man to hurt me so damn good again, and for every brutal dirty fuck yet to come.

THE END

Want More Sinful Santa Stories?

Check out:

Subbing for Santa: A Dark Christmas Romance
https://geni.us/subbingforsanta

Sinning for Santa: A Dark Mafia Christmas Romance
https://geni.us/sinningforsanta

ALSO BY SARAH JD

Sarah JD's Books

https://sarahjdauthor.com/books

STALK SARAH JD

WANT TO JOIN THE CONVERSATION ABOUT YOUR FAV CHARACTERS?

Join my Facebook Readers Group *SARAH'S VICIOUS KITTENS*
JOIN HERE! https://www.facebook.com/groups/sarahjaneduncanreadersgroup

For more information on books & book signing events please visit: https://sarahjdauthor.com

***

STALK SARAH HERE:

ABOUT THE AUTHOR

Sarah JD, also known as Sarah Jane Duncan, is an Australian dark romance author living her best life with her high school sweetheart, Mr Duncan.

Sarah can be found in her writing room plotting out her next smut filled romance, packed with angst, violence, and themes so dark you should probably question why you love it so much.

Sarah enjoys torturing her characters. There's nothing easy about their stories. They are hard, gritty, and painfully heartbreaking at times. But what doesn't kill us makes us stronger, right? And when you throw in a swoon worthy guy, or an alphahole you just want to slap, but also fall to your knees and obey, it's the recipe for a rollercoaster ride.

So buckle up. Read the warnings. And let yourself get lost in the dark stories Sarah creates.